Puppies
in a Puzzle

Dalmatian in the Dales

Illustrations by Ann Baum

Labrador on the Lawn

Illustrations by Ann Baum

LUCY DANIELS

Hodder
Children's
Books

A division of Hachette Children's Books

This bind-up edition published in 2012 by Hodder Children's Books

Thanks to C.J. Hall, B.Vet.Med., M.R.C.V.S. for reviewing the veterinary information contained in *Dalmation in the Dales*

Dalmatian in the Dales
Special thanks to Sue Bentley

Text copyright © 2002 Working Partners Limited
Illustrations copyright © 2002 Ann Baum
First published as a single volume in Great Britain in 2002
by Hodder Children's Books

Labrador on the Lawn
Special thanks to Ingrid Maitland

Text copyright © 2003 Working Partners Limited
Illustrations copyright © 2003 Ann Baum
First published as a single volume in Great Britain in 2003
by Hodder Children's Books

Animal Ark is a trademark of Working Partners Limited
Created by Working Partners Limited, London, WC1X 9HH
Original series created by Ben M. Baglio

The right of Lucy Daniels to be identified as the Author
of the Work has been asserted by her in accordance with
the Copyright, Designs and Patents Act 1988.

1

A Catalogue record for this book is available from the British Library

ISBN 978 1 444 91466 5

Typeset in Baskerville Book by Avon DataSet Ltd, Bidford-on-Avon

Printed and bound in Great Britain by Clays Ltd, St Ives plc

The paper and board used in this paperback by Hodder Children's Books
are natural recyclable products made from wood grown in sustainable
forests. The manufacturing processes conform to the environmental
regulations of the country of origin.

Hodder Children's Books
a division of Hachette Children's Books
338 Euston Road, London NW1 3BH
An Hachette UK company

www.hodderchildrens.co.uk

Dalmatian in the Dales

One

'Look over there!' Mandy Hope called to her best friend, James Hunter. She pointed across the moor to the edge of the woods.

'Hang on a minute! I've just got to get this shot.' James crouched down and pointed his camera at some rabbits in the distance, playing chase on the wind-blown slopes. 'Oh, they've all dived into their burrows.'

'Never mind! I've just seen something even better.' Mandy was hardly able to contain her excitement. 'Fallow deer!'

'Oh, wow! That's great!' James jumped up and pushed his glasses on to the bridge of his nose.

'Let's go!' Mandy set off up the hill, white limestone pebbles crunching beneath her boots. The sky was a clear brilliant blue over the rolling hills. Drystone walls snaked across acres of open space.

Normally, when she wasn't at school, Mandy helped out in her parents' veterinary surgery in Welford, but today was Saturday, and the surgery closed at lunchtime. Mandy and James had come to the moor to take photographs for the *Woodland Wildlife* magazine's competition.

'Those trees are the start of Glisterdale Forest,' Mandy said, as James fell into step with her. 'Honey-Mum and Sprite live there. I'd really love to see the two of them again.'

'Me too,' James agreed.

Honey-Mum was a fallow deer who had adopted the orphaned fawn.

'I bet Sprite has grown a lot by now,' Mandy said, thinking of the gentle fawn with her reddish-gold coat and light spots. She felt a pang as she remembered finding the tiny newborn bundle, helpless and alone behind the Old School House in Welford.

'She's been running free with the herd for months now,' said James. 'I wonder if we'll still recognise her?'

'I'd know her anywhere!' Mandy was confident. 'Besides, wasn't Sprite fitted with a blue ear tag?'

James grinned. 'Oh, yes. Well, that should help.'

Just inside the woods, they paused beneath a massive oak which was laden with fat green acorns. Mandy looked around, but could see no sign of the deer.

'They must have gone into the forest,' said James. He was probably right. But Mandy couldn't help feeling disappointed. She'd really been hoping to see Sprite and Honey-Mum again. Just then she noticed a narrow, flattened path that led through the bracken.

'Look – a deer trail. Come on, let's follow it!' Mandy started to push her way through the dry rust-coloured bracken.

James paused to fiddle with his camera. 'I'll put this on automatic focus. Then as soon as we catch sight of any deer, I'm ready for action.'

'OK,' Mandy said. James was brilliant with technical equipment. He knew all about light meters and lenses. They moved quietly down the trail. It led them into a grassy glade, bordered on all sides by trees. The spreading branches of one huge beech tree hung low enough to brush the grass.

'Lots of juicy shoots within reach. Just what deer like,' Mandy whispered. 'I reckon we might see some if we wait here.'

James nodded. 'This looks a good spot.' He crouched down to wait beside Mandy. All was quiet, except for the piping of a robin. A blackbird hopped into view and began foraging for grubs in the fallen leaves.

A few minutes passed, then Mandy stiffened. Stepping slowly into the autumn sunlight were five fallow deer. Mandy held her breath as she watched the group, three adult females and two fawns, make their way daintily across the grass. 'Aren't they beautiful!' she murmured. Her eyes flickered over the deers' rich, glossy chestnut coats. 'But I don't think any of those are Honey-Mum.'

'The light coming through the trees is perfect.' James was already raising his camera. 'Now – don't you move . . .'

Click. He pressed the button, just as the doe at the head of the group stopped and jerked her head round. She gave a sharp little bark, stamped her hoof and raised her tail to show the white fur underneath.

'She's warning them of danger,' Mandy said.

'Maybe they can smell us,' suggested James.

Mandy licked the tip of her finger and held it up. She shook her head. 'We're upwind of them. It's something else.'

'I don't see anything,' said James.

All at once the little herd took off. Leaping high over the grass, white tails bobbing, they headed for cover.

Suddenly there was a frantic rustling in the undergrowth to one side of them.

James spun round. 'What's that?'

'Oh!' Mandy's blue eyes widened as a large black and white dog came crashing through the bushes. 'It's a Dalmatian!'

The Dalmatian raced across the clearing. But it seemed to tire suddenly, and stopped, panting heavily. Mandy watched as it lifted up one front paw. She could see tremors moving over its black and white coat as its sides heaved. 'I think it's hurt its foot,' she said. She peered through the trees, expecting an owner with a lead to appear at any moment. But no one came.

'Maybe it's a stray?' suggested James.

Mandy shook her head doubtfully. 'A pedigree Dalmatian wouldn't be a stray. Besides, it looks too well-fed. And look – it's wearing a collar.'

'There might be a name and address on it,' said James.

'Good thinking,' Mandy replied. I'm going to see if I can make friends with it.'

She moved forward slowly. As she got closer she could see that the dog was a female. On one back leg, her spots formed an unusual shape just like a paw print. The Dalmatian's ears were laid flat against her head. Dipping her neck, she whined softly and licked her sore paw.

'Hello, girl,' Mandy said softly. 'Aren't you lovely?'

The dog didn't look up. Mandy frowned in concentration as she edged forward. Just a bit closer and she might be able to grab the collar. Slowly Mandy stretched out her hand.

The Dalmatian turned her head and seemed to see Mandy for the first time. She gave a violent start and jumped sideways. She looked ready to take off again at any moment.

'Don't be scared. I won't hurt you,' Mandy crooned. She made encouraging noises and rubbed her fingertips together.

The Dalmatian looked at her for a second with scared dark-brown eyes. Then she whined softly, turned tail and darted away through the trees.

James dashed after her. Mandy followed, but

she was only in time to see a black and white shape sprinting away into the distance. Soon it was no more than a speck between the trees.

'That dog really can run!' James puffed, stopping dead and resting his hands on his knees.

'You're not kidding!' Mandy's shoulders sagged. 'We hadn't a hope of catching her, even with a sore paw. Dad says Dalmatians can run all day without getting tired. They were bred to run beside carriages.'

'I wonder why that one seemed so exhausted then?' James mused.

Mandy frowned. 'That's a good point. Maybe she wasn't really tired, just lost and confused.'

'She was dead nervous. She nearly jumped out of her skin when she saw you,' James reminded her.

'I know. That was a bit strange too, wasn't it?' Mandy said. She was beginning to feel really worried about the dog. 'I hate to think of the poor thing out here all alone and injured.'

'Me too. I'd be worried sick if it was Blackie,' James said. Blackie was his boisterous young Labrador.

Mandy made up her mind. 'I think we should go after her and try to find her.'

'Me too. But where do we start?' asked James. 'We can't search the entire forest on foot. Besides, it will be starting to get dark soon.'

'That's true,' Mandy admitted. 'But we could search for a bit longer if we had some help. And a Land-rover . . .'

James caught on fast. 'Like your dad's?'

Mandy grinned. 'Exactly! I reckon he should have finished up at High Cross by now. He said he'd give us a lift home. Let's go and meet him.'

Mandy and James walked back along the road that curved around the edge of Glisterdale Forest. They had almost reached the stony track that led up to Lydia Fawcett's farm when the Animal Ark Land-rover appeared round a bend in front of them.

'Here's Dad!' Mandy raised her hand in a wave.

The Land-rover drew to a halt. 'Hi, you two,' said Adam Hope.

'Hi, Dad.' Mandy opened the door and jumped into the front seat.

James climbed into the back. 'Hello, Mr Hope.'

'How's Lydia? And Houdini?' Mandy asked. She always wanted to know all the details of her parents' visit to the local farms. Especially when it was to one of her friends.

'Lydia's fine. She said to say hello. One of her goats had broken a tooth,' her dad answered, grinning. 'And Houdini is his usual self, full of beans and getting into trouble.'

Mandy and James laughed. They knew all about Houdini. Lydia's favourite goat had been named after the famous escapologist.

'How did the wildlife photography go?' asked Adam Hope.

Mandy glanced over her shoulder at James. 'It kind of . . . didn't, did it James?'

'No. Not really,' admitted James.

Adam Hope checked his driver's mirror and edged the Land-rover away from the verge. 'Well, don't look so glum. There's still plenty of time to get your entries in.'

'We know. It's not that,' Mandy said, glancing at James. 'It's just that we were watching some deer when this Dalmatian came dashing through the woods. She seemed lost and we think she'd hurt her foot. So – if we're not in too much of a hurry to get back, I thought . . .'

'You want me to drive around the dales looking for it?' guessed her dad.

Mandy nodded. 'Can we?'

'Are you sure there wasn't an owner somewhere

in the woods?' Adam Hope asked. 'I know you, Mandy. Some animals just don't need rescuing!'

Mandy was almost certain that the dog had been alone, but she couldn't be sure. 'We didn't see anyone looking for their dog,' she said carefully.

'But the Dalmatian didn't look like a stray either,' James pointed out. 'It had a collar on.'

'Yes. Though I didn't get close enough to read any details,' Mandy rushed on. 'And I'm sure she had hurt her foot, Dad. Even though she ran off again . . .'

'Whoa! OK, you two! I'm convinced!' Adam Hope held his hands up and grinned at Mandy. 'You'd better show me where she was heading.'

'Thanks, Dad!' she breathed.

Mandy directed her dad to the edge of the woods where she and James had last seen the Dalmatian. Mr Hope drove up and down the road, but there was no sign of her.

'Maybe we should call into some of the car parks?' suggested James. 'Lots of dog-walkers use them.'

'Good idea,' Mandy said. 'I'll ask anyone if they've seen a Dalmatian.'

But even though they spoke to several ramblers who were just returning to their car, no one had seen a lone Dalmatian.

Half an hour later, Mr Hope pulled to a halt. 'There's a lot of space round here to cover,' he said. 'That dog could be anywhere by now.'

Mandy stared out at the winding road. Even she had to admit to feeling discouraged. The light over the dales was beginning to fade now. The sky had turned to violet and tiny lights glimmered from the hill farms on the steep slopes.

'I think it's time we went home,' Adam Hope said.

'OK.' Mandy admitted defeat. 'Thanks for looking, anyway, Dad.'

'Yes, thanks, Mr Hope,' said James.

'No problem.' Adam Hope switched on the headlights. 'There may have been an owner around, even if you and James didn't see one. I wouldn't be surprised if your Dalmatian isn't tucked up warm at home by now.'

'I hope so,' Mandy said, but she wasn't convinced. For some reason that she couldn't explain to herself, she felt sure that the Dalmatian was out there somewhere, hurt and frightened and probably hungry too. She stared gloomily ahead at the road as they sped down the valley.

Adam Hope began to sing. 'All things bright and beautiful . . .' His rich baritone voice filled the car.

Despite herself, Mandy smiled. Her dad was in the church choir and he had a habit of bursting into song at any time. She glanced at James in the mirror and rolled her eyes. Her dad could be so embarrassing.

But James just shrugged and grinned.

'. . . all things wise and wonderful . . .' Mr Hope continued the hymn. 'My tummy tells me it's almost supper time. Macaroni cheese tonight. With lots of toasted cheese on top.'

'Da-ad!' Mandy protested. 'What about your diet?'

'I'm on a new one now. It's called the seafood diet.' Her dad grinned, a glint in his eye.

Mandy groaned. 'I know. You see-food and you eat it, right? That's a terrible joke!'

Adam Hope pretended to look hurt. Mandy and James laughed.

The Land-rover's engine changed tone as they sped up out of the valley. Mandy began to think of the animals she was going to check on as soon as she got back to Animal Ark. Animals that were too sick to go home were kept in the residential unit overnight. At the moment there was a kitten with a broken leg and a rabbit which had had an operation to remove a tumour.

Just then, Mr Hope's mobile phone rang.

He pulled over to the side of the road before answering. 'Hello? Oh, Mr Western. What can I do for you?'

Sam Western's loud voice came out of the mobile. Mandy and James caught a few words of what he was saying.

'Just happened . . . get over here, man. Now!'

Mandy glanced over her shoulder at James. What was Sam Western up to? The tough local businessman owned the woods where they had just been. He had no love of wildlife and ran his farms strictly for profit.

'Try and calm down,' Mr Hope was saying into the mobile. 'Just tell me what happened.' His good-natured face became serious as he listened.

'Sounds bad,' James hissed to Mandy.

Adam Hope spoke calmly, his brow furrowed in concentration. 'OK. I understand. Now – tell me where you are. Good, I'm quite near to you. I'll be there in a few minutes.'

Mandy waited tensely for her dad to finish speaking. 'What's wrong, Dad?' she asked.

'We have to go straight back up to Glisterdale,' her dad replied, as he checked the road in his driving mirror. 'Hang on, you two.' He swung the

Land-rover into a nearby gateway and turned round.

'What's going on?' Mandy asked, a cold feeling creeping over her.

'It's one of Sam Western's bulldogs, Boris,' Adam Hope explained. 'He's been shot.'

'What!' Mandy felt shocked. She completely forgot her dislike of the dog's owner, she was so upset for the dog. 'Poor Boris,' she gasped. Her mind whirled. Who would shoot a dog?

Two

'There's Sam Western's car by the lamppost!' Mandy leaned forward in her seat as her father drew into the car park. In the headlights, she caught sight of Sam Western kneeling on the ground. A bulky white shape was lying on a rug beside him. It was Boris. The bulldog's back legs were streaked with blood, and he wasn't moving.

'Oh no,' Mandy gasped.

As Adam Hope parked the Land-rover and got out, Sam Western stood up. His grey-blond hair stuck up in tufts where he'd run his hands through it.

'Thank goodness you're here!' said Mr Western.

Mr Hope went straight over to the injured dog and knelt down. 'Mandy, would you get my bag, please?' he called over his shoulder.

'OK, Dad.' Mandy hurried to fetch it from the back of the Land-rover. She dashed back with it and handed it to her dad. 'Here you are.'

'Thanks, love.' Adam Hope ran his expert hands over Boris. After a few moments, he looked up. 'These are gunshot wounds all right, Mr Western. There are pellets embedded in his back legs.'

Mandy felt her stomach lurch.

'What happened exactly?' Adam Hope asked.

Sam Western looked impatient. 'It's like I said. I let Boris off for a run in the woods. Then I came and sat in my Land-rover. I had a couple of calls to make. Next thing I know, Boris has come back and he's got blood on him. When I think back, I might have heard shots, but I was on the phone and I didn't take much notice. I thought it was probably one of the farmers shooting rabbits.'

'Did you have a look around for someone you might recognise?' Mr Hope asked.

Sam Western shook his head. 'I was too worried about Boris. The minute I saw what had happened, I phoned you.'

Adam Hope nodded sympathetically. 'That's

understandable. I think Boris has been very lucky. Some of these wounds are quite deep, but he should be all right. I'll need to take him back to the surgery to do X-rays before I remove the pellets.'

'Is that to check for any damage to the bone?' Mandy asked.

Her dad nodded. 'And I want to make sure that no major blood vessels have been ruptured.'

'Never mind all the questions.' Sam Western elbowed James aside. 'Can't you do something for him now? Look at him – he's trembling all over.'

'That's due to the shock.' Adam Hope got Mandy to pass him a bottle and a sterile packet, containing a syringe. I'm going to give him something for that right now.'

'Poor boy,' Mandy said soothingly to Boris. 'This will make you feel better.'

Boris lifted his big square head. Mandy saw that his dark eyes were clouded with pain. Lifting one of his wrinkled jowls, he gave a soft growl.

'Be careful, Mandy,' warned her dad.

'I know, Dad,' Mandy replied. She understood that animals could be unpredictable when they were in pain.

Sam Western frowned. 'Do we have to have these kids getting in the way?'

'It's OK, Mandy's used to helping in the surgery,' said Adam Hope. 'And if they hadn't persuaded me to stay up at the dales, I'd have taken a lot longer to get to you and Boris.'

Sam Western ignored him. 'I'll hold Boris's collar while you give him the injection.'

Mandy and James watched as Sam Western took hold of Boris's steel-studded collar. 'It's all right, boy,' he said gruffly, smoothing the dog's ear. Boris gave a feeble bark and tried to lick his owner's hand.

Mr Hope injected Boris in the loose skin at his neck. Then he asked Mandy to pass him some antiseptic swabs and dressings.

Mr Western patted Boris's head as the dog gave a faint yelp of pain. 'Just wait until I get my hands on whoever did this!' he muttered.

Mandy thought she had never seen Mr Western looking so pale and shaken. Whatever his faults, he was certainly fond of his dog.

Once Boris was more comfortable, Sam Western turned to Mr Hope. 'I think it could have been poachers who shot Boris,' he said abruptly.

'What makes you think that?' asked Mr Hope.

'The shots I heard came from deep in the woods,' Sam Western replied. 'Farmers shoot rabbits out in the open. I'd have thought of it earlier if I hadn't been so worried about Boris.'

'Poachers!' Mandy threw a horrified glance at James.

James looked equally shaken by the news.

'It's certainly a possibility,' said Adam Hope. He looked across at Mandy and James. 'Did you two see anything suspicious when you were up here taking photographs this afternoon? Any people you didn't recognise?'

Mandy shook her head. 'No. We didn't see anyone, did we, James?'

'Just the Dalmatian,' answered James.

'Poachers are hardly going to advertise themselves though,' Sam Western said shortly.

Poachers! Horrible images of animals being hunted crowded Mandy's head. And what about the deer? Would they be all right? The thought of beautiful gentle Sprite or Honey-Mum lying dead was unbearable.

'I think you're going to need hard evidence that it was poachers before you alert the authorities,' Adam Hope warned Mr Western.

'Well, it's pretty obvious what happened, isn't it?' Sam Western replied. 'Boris got in someone's way when they were shooting at my deer. Why else would anyone be deep in the woods with rifles?'

'I'd say you were probably right,' Adam Hope said reasonably. 'But I don't think we can be certain at this stage.'

Mandy's head came up. As her dad said, there was no proof that it was poachers who had injured Boris. She had a sudden idea. 'Dad? Do you need me to help you any more?'

'No, you're all right,' Adam Hope answered.

'Mr Western can help me put Boris into the back of the Land-rover.'

'So James and I have got time to have a quick look around?' Mandy asked.

Mr Hope took a look at his daughter's determined face. 'OK. But be careful and you'll have to be quick. I want to get Boris back to the unit pretty soon.'

'OK, Dad.' Mandy sprang towards the Land-rover. 'Come on,' she called to James.

'Where are we going?' James raised his eyebrows.

'To get some torches from the Land-rover. Dad always keeps some for night call-outs.' She found the torches and passed one to James. 'If it was poachers who shot Boris they might have left some signs.'

It was dark under the trees, away from the car headlights. Overhead, the first stars were out. Somewhere in the forest an owl hooted.

Mandy and James shone the powerful torches on to the ground. Twigs crunched beneath their trainers as they looked around.

'Seen anything yet?' Mandy whispered.

James shook his head. 'Just a few fir cones and some toadstools.'

'What we need is to find where Boris was shot,'

Mandy decided. 'Maybe we'll find an empty cartridge or something.'

'Good thinking. Hang on.' James paused briefly and began working things through logically. 'Look – Western parked over there, OK? He told us that Boris came running from that direction. So I reckon that it has to be somewhere around here that Boris was injured.'

'Sounds good to me,' Mandy said, swinging her torch.

The powerful beam of yellow light played over the moss-covered logs and patches of nettles. Taking small steps, Mandy quickly worked her way around the small clearing. Then she saw something glinting in a pile of leaves. 'James, over here!' she called excitedly. 'I think I've found something!'

'What is it?' James hurried over to her side as Mandy crouched down.

Mandy brushed the damp leaves aside and her fingers closed over a blue plastic tube with a metal cap at the closed end. An empty gun cartridge!

'Look!' She held it up for James to see.

James swung his torch in an arc over a nearby patch of leaves. He gave a cry of triumph. 'There are more of them over here.'

'This is the proof Mr Western needs!' Mandy

slipped the empty cartridges into the pocket of her jeans.

'Not exactly.' James frowned. 'It proves that someone has been firing a gun, but Sam Western already said that a farmer might have been shooting rabbits or something.'

'Oh, yes.' Mandy's face fell. 'And he sells permits for people to shoot pigeons on his estate, doesn't he?'

James nodded. 'If we want to prove that these were deer poachers we need to find some more evidence.'

'Like what?'

'Like . . . that!' Suddenly James leaped forward. 'Look over there!'

Mandy shone her torch in the direction James had indicated. The impressions were marked in the dark soft ground. Tyre tracks.

'These are really clear!' Mandy went and stood beside James. 'And footprints, too. More than two men. You can see the different patterns of the boots.'

'You would need a van for poaching large animals,' James pointed out.

Mandy shivered. It looked as if their worst suspicions might be confirmed.

'Let's go back and tell your dad and Sam Western,' said James.

Mandy and James emerged into the car park to find that Boris was safely in the back of the Land-rover.

'It looks like Mr Western was right about poachers,' Mandy said to her dad. 'We found these!' She held out the empty cartridges.

'And there are tyre marks and lots of footprints back there,' added James. 'It looks like there were three or four men.'

'Good work, you two,' said Adam Hope.

'Right,' Sam Western said grimly. 'I'd better stay and have a scout round here. I want to have a closer look at the evidence.'

'If you take my advice, you'll get some back-up,' said Mr Hope.

'Don't worry, I will. I'll call Dennis and get him to bring a couple of men over here.' Dennis Saville was Sam Western's estate manager. 'Make sure you look after Boris,' Mr Western added gruffly. 'Money's no object. I want him to have the best treatment.'

'All our patients get the best treatment,' Mandy was stung into replying.

Her dad put a hand on her shoulder. 'It's

all right, love,' he said softly.

Sam Western ignored Mandy's outburst. 'I'll call in to check on Boris in the morning,' he said shortly. He turned on his heel and strode away. Then he stopped and looked back for a moment. 'Er – well done, both of you,' he said grudgingly to Mandy and James.

'Coming from Sam Western, that's praise indeed!' said Adam Hope with a broad grin as he opened the Land-rover's door.

Mandy shrugged. She didn't care about being thanked. She just hoped that the poachers would be caught. Then Honey-Mum, Sprite, and the other deer would be safe.

The journey home passed swiftly on the empty roads, and shortly Adam Hope drew up in Welford village. James got out and went towards his house. 'Thanks for the lift, Mr Hope. See you tomorrow, Mandy,' he called.

It was completely dark by the time Adam Hope pulled into the Hopes' front drive, past the wooden sign which read, 'Animal Ark, Veterinary Surgery'. He opened the car's back door and reached for Boris who was wrapped snugly in a blanket. 'Oof! This is one heavy dog,' he groaned.

'I'll help,' Mandy said.

Boris gave a rumbling growl and snapped at the air.

'Watch your fingers,' warned Mandy's dad.

They made their way carefully around to the red brick surgery attached to the back of the cottage.

Emily Hope popped her head round the door. Her curly red hair was tied back and she wore a fleece top, loose trousers, and trainers. 'Hello! I saw you arrive from the window. Isn't that one of Sam Western's dogs?'

'Hi, Mum!' Mandy said. 'Yes, it's Boris. Have you got a yoga class?'

'Yes. I was just leaving,' answered Emily Hope. She held the door open so that Mandy and Adam Hope could carry the dog inside.

'So how is it that you and James go out taking photographs and come back with a bulldog?' Mrs Hope asked.

While Boris was settled gently on the treatment room table, Mandy told her mum about Boris getting shot and the evidence she and James had found.

'Poachers? That's bad news.' Emily Hope grew serious as she listened.

Mr Hope nodded in agreement. 'These gangs are pretty organised nowadays. A lot of them are town based. Western's going to have his work cut out trying to track them down.'

'I expect he'll have notified the police by now,' said Emily Hope. 'Do you need a hand with Boris?'

Adam Hope shook his head. 'No. It's all right. Mandy can help me. You go to your class.'

'OK. If you're sure.' Mrs Hope dropped a brief kiss on Mandy's head. 'See you two later.'

In the treatment room, Adam Hope scrubbed his hands at the sink. Boris was trying to move around in his blanket.

'Poor boy,' Mandy soothed. 'Dad will soon make you better.'

Boris answered with a deep growl.

Mandy's dad reached into a cupboard. 'I'm just going to give this grumpy chap a bit more sedative before we see to him.'

'Good idea,' Mandy said. 'Isn't it a shame that injured animals don't always understand that we're trying to help them?'

Her dad nodded. 'It would certainly be useful to talk to the animals sometimes! Right,' Adam Hope went on, 'Boris is nice and relaxed now. I'll do the X-rays.'

There was a short wait while the X-rays were developed. Then Adam Hope pinned them up and switched on the light box. Mandy could see Boris's short strong leg bones, surrounded by about ten small white marks. 'Are those the pellets?' she pointed.

'Yes,' answered her dad. 'See how they've lodged in the muscles and missed the bone and major blood vessels? Boris is a very lucky dog.'

'Will his legs be all right?' Mandy asked.

'They should be. He's a strong healthy dog. But those are nasty wounds. I'll want to keep an eye on him for a day or two. Now, let's remove those pellets.'

Mandy washed her hands while her dad worked on Boris. Carefully, she took instruments from the sterilising unit and handed them to him.

'There. That's the last one,' Adam Hope said finally, straightening up. He opened the long, blunt-ended tweezers and the pellet clanged into a metal dish.

Mandy stroked Boris's wrinkled forehead. He was breathing deeply now and making loud rattling snorts.

'Isn't he noisy?' Mandy said, as her dad finished dressing Boris's wounds. 'He's going to keep all the other animals in the unit awake!'

'Bulldogs tend to snore loudly,' said Adam Hope, removing his rubber gloves. 'It's because they have pushed-back jaws and snub noses.'

Mandy's eyes sparkled. 'So what's your excuse for snoring, Dad?'

'Cheek!' Adam Hope pretended to look hurt. 'There's no respect for the older generation these days . . .' he added mournfully.

Mandy laughed and gave him an affectionate dig in the ribs.

'Boris is going to need a course of antibiotics,' said her dad, unlocking the medication cupboard.

'Not tablets, surely?' Mandy queried. She didn't envy anyone trying to get tablets down Boris's throat.

Mr Hope chuckled at the look on her face. 'Don't worry. I'll give him an injection now, then he can have drops in his food.'

'Phew! That's a relief,' Mandy said. 'Shall I help you settle him in the unit?'

Together they lifted the heavy, sleepy bulldog and took him through to the residential unit at the back of the extension. It smelt faintly of lemon disinfectant.

Mandy spread a cosy blanket in an empty cage.

Then she filled a water bowl. 'There, Boris,' she said softly. 'You'll feel much better when you wake up.'

The only reply was a loud snore.

Mandy checked that the other animals had clean bedding, food and water. As she finally headed for the Animal Ark kitchen she realised that she was really hungry. It had been an eventful day, what with the deer, then Boris and the poachers . . . and then there had been the Dalmatian, too. With everything else, Mandy had almost forgotten about her.

Now Mandy began to worry again. Had the nervous dog found her way home? Or was she spending the night alone out on the bleak, dark moors? Mandy shivered. She didn't like the thought of that – especially not now there was the added danger of poachers.

Three

'Supper's ready!' Adam Hope lifted two steaming dishes out of the oven. 'There's garlic bread too.'

Mandy ground black pepper on to the tomato salad she had just made, then sat down at the table.

'Just what the doctor ordered.' Mr Hope began dishing out macaroni cheese.

'Don't you mean just what the vet ordered?' Mandy joked.

As they began to eat, Emily Hope came in. 'Mmm. It smells wonderful in here. All that yoga has given me an appetite.'

'I thought yoga was supposed to relax you,' Mandy said.

'That's right,' said her mum with a grin, her freckles seeming to dance across her nose. She sat down next to Mandy. 'I'm relaxed and starving.'

They all laughed.

'How's Boris?' asked Mrs Hope.

Her husband swallowed his mouthful of food before answering. 'He's resting in the unit. Mandy was pretty impressed by his loud snores, weren't you, love?'

'Uh-huh,' Mandy murmured absently, her mind back on the Dalmatian. She had only eaten a few mouthfuls and was now pushing the food around on her plate.

Emily Hope tapped Mandy's arm gently. 'Come on. Out with it.'

'What?' Mandy looked up in surprise.

'Whatever's on your mind,' her mum prompted.

'I think I know what it is,' said Mr Hope. 'You're still worried about that Dalmatian, aren't you?'

'Dalmatian?' Emily Hope blinked. 'Correct me if I'm wrong, but I thought we were just talking about a bulldog!'

Mandy couldn't help laughing at her mum's puzzled expression. 'We were! But before we found out about Boris, James and I saw a Dalmatian running around the forest, all by herself. She seemed really nervous and I think her leg was injured.'

'Mandy persuaded me to drive around looking for her but we couldn't see any sign,' Mr Hope put in. 'I feel pretty sure that she's been reunited with her owner by now.'

'But you don't agree?' Emily Hope asked her daughter.

'No. Not really,' Mandy admitted. 'There was something a bit unusual about that dog.' She bit her lip, not sure how to explain why she felt so worried. 'She seemed so . . . spooked.'

'You're sure your imagination's not just working overtime?' Emily Hope asked gently.

Mandy blushed. She knew that she had a tendency to leap to conclusions sometimes, especially where animals were concerned. 'I don't think so. But I'll feel better when James and I have been back up to Glisterdale to look for her again tomorrow . . .' She tailed off, having caught the look that passed between her parents.

'I don't think that's a good idea,' said her mum. 'I'd rather you kept right away from those woods until the poachers have been caught.'

'Oh, Mum . . .' Mandy groaned. She cast a pleading glance at her father. Sometimes she could get round him more easily.

But he shook his head too. 'I'm afraid I agree with your mother. It's just too dangerous. You've seen what's happened to Boris.'

Mandy opened her mouth to speak.

'No buts, Mandy,' Emily Hope said firmly. 'I want you to promise that you'll stay away from those woods.'

'OK. I promise.' Mandy's shoulders slumped. She knew when she was beaten.

After supper, she helped clear and wash the dishes. Then she decided to go up to her bedroom. She had a bit more to do on her holiday homework and the new term started in a few days.

'Need any help with your small mammals project?' asked her mum.

'No thanks,' Mandy replied. 'I've just got a few pictures left to do.'

'All right,' Emily Hope looked concerned. 'See you later then. And try not to worry about that Dalmatian.' She gave Mandy a warm understanding smile.

Mandy went upstairs and pushed back the door to her room. She loved its low ceiling and the thick dark beam running across it. She felt herself relax as she began setting out paper and coloured pencils.

For an hour she sat at the table by the window and enjoyed making a detailed drawing of a field mouse. A few last delicate strokes to the fur and it was finished. She held up the drawing and sighed. The mouse's head was wonky and its eyes looked slightly crossed. 'It's not brilliant, but it's not too bad,' she muttered, pulling a face.

After tidying away her pencils, she went downstairs to say goodnight to her parents. She found them in the sitting room. Her mum was sitting by the fireplace, reading a vet's magazine, while her dad was watching TV.

' 'Night, Mum. 'Night, Dad,' said Mandy.

'Goodnight,' replied her parents. 'Sleep tight.'

It was warm and cosy under her duvet, but Mandy lay awake for a long time, thinking about deer and poachers and an exhausted Dalmatian, foot-sore and weary, spending a lonely night out on the dales.

'OK. I give in,' said Mr Hope first thing the following morning.

'What?' Mandy frowned.

'I know what those dark circles under your eyes mean, Mandy Hope,' Adam Hope went on. 'So if you and James want to go up to Glisterdale to look for that Dalmatian again, it's all right with me and your Mum.'

'Really?' Mandy flew across the kitchen to give him a hug. 'Thanks, Dad. That's brilliant!'

'Not so fast.' Emily Hope popped her head around the kitchen door. 'There is one condition.'

'Oh!' Mandy's face fell. That sounded like trouble.

'You have to take me with you,' her mum said, her eyes sparkling.

'Great! I can't think of a better way to spend a Sunday morning!' Mandy danced on the spot.

'And you have to do your usual chores first,' Adam Hope added, trying to sound strict.

'I'm already on my way,' Mandy sang out, halfway through the door. 'I'll just give James a ring first to tell him we'll pick him up!'

In the unit, Boris's muscular body was slumped in one corner. His bandaged back legs stuck out awkwardly. He gave a gruff complaining bark when Mandy went up to him.

'Poor you. Still feeling sore?' Mandy said

sympathetically. To her surprise Boris wagged his stumpy rosette of a tail. She felt bold enough to put a finger through the wire mesh and scratch his wrinkled forehead. Boris watched her for a few seconds. Then his black eyes narrowed and he gave a soft growl.

'OK, I get the message,' Mandy said, moving away. She usually reckoned she could get on with any animal, but Boris looked like being the exception.

She quickly filled water and food bowls and changed litter trays. The important work over, she set about wiping surfaces and mopping the floor at double speed.

'Finished!' she declared. 'Time for Operation Dalmatian!' Dashing through into the cottage, she went to find her boots and anorak.

'All things bright and beautiful . . .' Adam Hope sang out.

Mandy grimaced as she darted out to the front drive. 'Have a good choir practice, Dad! See you later.'

'By-eee!' came the long deep note.

Mandy climbed in beside her mum and they went to pick up James.

The roads were clear, and it wasn't long before Mrs Hope was driving the Land-rover up the winding road across the moors. Strands of grey mist hung low around the fields, bleaching the colours from the trees and hedges.

'OK. Over to you two. Where do we start looking for this elusive Dalmatian?' asked Emily Hope.

Mandy gave her mum directions. 'Last time we saw it, it was hurtling through the woods up near Upper Welford Hall.'

Mrs Hope shifted the car's gears. 'The woods it is, then.'

Mandy kept her eyes peeled for any sign of the Dalmatian. She felt herself grow tense as they reached the woods where Boris had been shot. She peered anxiously into the trees at the side of the road. Glancing in the car's mirror, she saw that James looked worried too.

But there was no sign of any gang of men with guns, and no sign of a lone dog either.

'Maybe we should widen the search,' suggested Emily Hope after an hour of fruitless driving through the forest. 'Shall we try looking on the moors?'

Mandy and James agreed. As her mum drove on, Mandy's eyes roved over every bare ridge, and every stretch of stony hillside. The moors were covered with stunted grass and tough, spiky gorse. 'There's nowhere here for a dog to shelter,' she pointed out. She tried to imagine what she would do if she were a dog. Where would she go to find warmth and shelter? A barn? A stable? Well, a farm had those things. 'I think we should check out any farms,' she decided.

James pointed down to the valley bottom. A cluster of grey buildings nestled there behind some trees. 'That's the first one we've seen.'

'Let's try it then.' Mrs Hope steered the Land-rover into the farmyard and stopped outside the farmhouse. 'We'd better go and ask if it's OK for us to look around.'

She got out and went to knock on the door. Mandy and James went with her. A man answered almost at once.

'Good morning. We're looking for a Dalmatian. Have you seen one?' Emily Hope asked the farmer.

'No, haven't seen anything on four legs around here except my sheep. But you're welcome to look around,' the farmer said. 'I hope you find your dog.'

'Oh, it's not our dog,' Mandy said.

'We think it might be a stray,' James added.

'Oh, aye. Well good luck anyway.' The farmer nodded to them and went back inside.

Mandy, her mum and James looked round the farmyard. They checked the barns, feed sheds and garages, but there was nothing. Mandy let out a discouraged sigh and put her hands on her hips, gazing out across the fields.

Where else was there to look? Suddenly she caught sight of an old stone barn. There were holes in the roof and the door hung off its hinges

at an awkward angle. 'I'm going to look over there!' she called to James and her mum.

Her feet pounded against the grass as she ran. As she reached the barn, she slowed down and went quietly inside. She breathed in the scent of dust, dried leaves and old straw. Daylight shining in through holes in the roof illuminated the dusky gloom.

Wooden pens stood against the far wall. Mandy looked more closely. What was that? It looked as though there was something curled up tight in one of them. Now it was looking at her with wide scared eyes.

It was the Dalmatian!

'Oh!' Mandy breathed. 'We've found you at last!'

She bent down to make herself seem smaller and less threatening as she began moving slowly towards the frightened dog. 'Hello, again. You must be hungry and cold,' she murmured.

The Dalmatian kept her eyes on Mandy's face. She licked her lips nervously and rose unsteadily to her feet.

Mandy's mum and James appeared in the doorway. Mandy looked over her shoulder and signalled to them not to make any sudden moves. She could see by their faces that they understood.

'Take care, Mandy,' Emily Hope said a low voice. 'She seems very scared.'

Mandy nodded. She knew that dogs could sometimes bite in fear as well as in anger.

The Dalmatian stood there trembling. It stared into her face as she held her hand out for it to sniff.

'It's OK, we're here to help you,' she said softly. Mandy held her breath. For a moment, she thought that the dog was going to run away again, then its long tail began to wag and a cold nose brushed against her fingers.

'It's all right! She wants to be friends,' she called over her shoulder to her mum and James. 'Aren't you a sweetheart?' she added as she stroked the dog's muscular chest.

James and Mrs Hope came over and crouched down next to Mandy.

'Isn't she lovely?' James fondled the Dalmatian's spotted ears. But as his hand brushed against the dog's head, she whined and drew back.

Emily Hope frowned. 'It looks like she has some tenderness there. And she seems unsteady on her feet. Keep talking to her, Mandy. I'll check her over.'

Mandy and James watched as Mrs Hope examined the dog.

'Oh,' Mandy gasped, when her mum lifted one of the dog's feet. 'Her pads are all cracked and sore.'

Mrs Hope nodded. 'She's covered a long distance on those. But they'll soon heal. I'm more puzzled by this lump on her head. It seems to be an older injury.'

'How could she have hurt her head?' asked James.

'It's hard to say without knowing anything about her,' replied Emily Hope. 'I'll have a closer look when we get her back to Animal Ark. But just now I want to give her some fluids. She's very dehydrated.'

Mandy nipped back to the Land-rover to fetch her mum's bag. 'There we are,' said Mrs Hope, giving the dog an injection. 'That'll make you feel better. Now, let's get you back to the surgery and on to a drip.'

Just then a voice came floating into the barn. It was a girl calling out a name, over and over again. 'Echo! Echo!' The voice cracked on a sob. 'Oh, Echo! Where are you?'

Mandy and James looked at each other. 'You don't think she's looking for this Dalmatian, do you?' said James.

'Let's go and see!' Mandy urged.

They leaped to their feet and ran over to the open barn door. Just as they reached it, a girl came running up. She looked about thirteen. Her face was white and tear-stained.

Then Mandy saw her catch sight of Mrs Hope kneeling down next to the exhausted dog. The girl gave a trembling smile and her whole face seemed to light up with relief.

'Echo!' she breathed. 'It really is you. Where have you been?'

Four

Mandy watched as the girl ran straight over and threw her arms round the Dalmatian's neck. 'I've been so worried about you,' she murmured. Echo gave a short bark and licked her owner's face.

'She seems really pleased to see you,' Mandy said.

'Yes. She does, doesn't she?' The girl beamed and dried her eyes. She had long dark hair and an open friendly face. 'I'm Julia Hampton,' she said. 'And Echo's my dog. She ran off while we were out for a walk,' she explained, stroking the Dalmatian's ears over and over.

Mandy liked Julia at once. 'Hi, I'm Mandy

Hope,' she said. 'And this is James Hunter.'

'Hi,' said James.

Julia seemed to notice the open vet's bag on the floor for the first time. She glanced at Emily Hope in alarm.

'My mum and dad are vets,' Mandy explained quickly. 'Mum was just giving Echo some emergency treatment.'

Julia's face fell. 'Is something wrong with Echo?'

'Nothing that we can't fix,' Mrs Hope said reassuringly. 'She's exhausted and dehydrated and those sore paws are going to need some attention, but we'll soon have her right.'

The strained look was fading from around Julia's eyes. 'Thank you so much for finding Echo and looking after her.'

'You have Mandy and James here to thank for that,' said Emily Hope. 'They saw your dog running on the dales yesterday and were worried about who she belonged to. The two of them wouldn't give up until we had searched every last bit of Glisterdale.'

'Really?' Julia looked surprised and grateful. She turned to Mandy and James. 'That's brilliant.'

'That's OK,' they answered. James, shy as usual, blushed.

Emily Hope laughed. 'Once you get to know these two, you'll understand. They never give up if they think an animal needs rescuing.'

'Lucky for me and Echo then!' said Julia. 'I don't really know what happened yesterday. I was taking Echo for a walk on the moors when she ran away. I called her and called her, but she didn't come back. She's run off once before, but this is the first time she's stayed out all night.'

'Sounds like Echo needs a few obedience lessons,' Emily Hope said gently. 'Has she always been like that?'

Julia shook her head. 'No. She used to be so lovely and good-natured. Mum used to say that she was my shadow – she went everywhere with me. But now she seems so jumpy all the time. She even snapped at me the other day.'

'But Echo seems like such a lovely gentle dog,' Mandy said.

'She soon made friends with us, didn't she?' James added.

Mandy nodded. 'And she must have been in pain as well as feeling scared and confused, but she didn't snap or anything.'

'That's true, love,' her mum said thoughtfully. She looked at Julia. 'How odd that Echo's temperament has changed so drastically. It must be very difficult for you and your family.'

'It is!' Julia's eyes filled with tears. 'Mum and Dad are fed up with her running away and being so nervous and snappy. They want to find her a new home.'

'Oh, no!' Mandy felt really sorry for Julia. She obviously loved Echo and wanted to keep her pet.

Mrs Hope gave Julia a tissue. She patted her arm. 'Things might not be as bad as they look. They rarely are. Come on, I'd like to get Echo back to Animal Ark – that's our veterinary surgery. You should come too.'

'I'll have to tell my parents where I am,' said Julia. 'We live near here. They know I'm looking for Echo, but they'll be worried if I'm back late.'

'That's OK. You can use Mum's mobile to call your parents,' Mandy suggested. 'Couldn't she, Mum?'

Mrs Hope nodded. 'Of course. Tell them that you can come in the Land-rover with Echo. Maybe they could meet you at Animal Ark?'

'OK. Thanks.' Julia made her call, then she handed the mobile back to Emily Hope, her expression downcast. 'They said they'll meet me at the surgery.'

'What's wrong?' Mandy asked.

Julia shrugged. She looked up at Mandy, her face white and set. 'Mum and Dad didn't say anything, but I can tell they're not too thrilled that I've found Echo. She's just too much trouble, you see? They probably wish that Echo had run off and had never come back!'

Back at Animal Ark, the Hamptons had driven over to meet their daughter. They stood with sombre expressions in the treatment room, where Echo lay on the table.

As Mrs Hope treated Echo, Julia stroked the Dalmatian.

'Be careful, Julia. Echo might snap at you,' Mrs Hampton warned her daughter. Mandy thought Julia's mum sounded more worried about Echo than annoyed.

But the strong muscular dog only licked her owner's hand gently. 'She's fine now, Mum,' Julia smiled.

Mandy frowned. It was hard to believe that this was the same problem dog Julia had described.

'Hmm. I'm still puzzled by that lump on her head,' said Mrs Hope. 'It seems sore, but there's no broken skin, so I think I'll leave well alone.'

She went over to the sink to wash her hands. 'Echo's much calmer after the sedative I've given her and her paws will feel a lot more comfortable soon. But she's still very dehydrated. I'd like to keep her here on a drip overnight.'

'Is that OK?' Julia asked her parents.

'Of course it is, darling,' said Julia's mum. 'Echo means the world to you, doesn't she?' Mrs Hampton gave her daughter a hug. She had brown hair like Julia's, but worn short and spiky.

Julia glared at her mother and pulled away. 'So why do you want to find her a new home?' she demanded.

Mrs Hampton looked a little uncomfortable. 'You know we don't want to do that, love. But if Echo keeps running off and being so unpredictable, we might have no choice.'

Julia tossed her dark hair over her shoulder. She seemed about to protest again.

'I find it's better not to make these kind of decisions in haste,' Emily Hope said quickly, in her warm sensible way. 'Why don't we wait and see how Echo is after a day or so?'

Julia gave her a grateful smile. 'OK.'

'That's a very good idea,' Mr Hampton agreed.

'And don't worry about Echo,' Mandy said to

Julia. 'I'll make sure she's all right.'

'Mandy keeps an eye on all the patients in the residential unit,' Mrs Hope explained.

Echo gave a soft bark and wagged her tail.

'She's saying that she feels a lot better,' Julia said confidently, running a hand over Echo's head.

Mr and Mrs Hampton managed a smile but Mandy could see that they still looked worried. Julia gave Echo a final cuddle, then left for home with her parents.

'What's that terrible noise?' James followed Mandy and Emily Hope, as they led Echo through to the unit.

Loud rumbling sounds filled the spotless room which was lined with wire cages. In one of them a squat white shape lay flat on its tummy, with its front legs sticking out straight. Boris!

Mandy chuckled. 'That's him – snoring!'

James looked impressed. 'Wow! I bet that would register on a decibel meter!'

'A what?' Mandy said, puzzled.

'A machine that measures sound levels,' said James.

'Poor old Echo is never going to get any rest with that noise,' Mandy observed.

'Or any other patient either!' Mrs Hope said with a smile as another rattling snore filled the air.

Mandy and James chuckled. 'You have to see the funny side!' Mandy pointed out.

She helped make Echo comfortable in a large cage. Echo turned round a couple of times, then curled up on the clean blanket. She put her nose between her paws and seemed to fall asleep straight away.

'Amazing!' Mandy said. 'She must be really exhausted if not even that racket can disturb her.'

Just then a familiar figure in a tweed jacket appeared at the entrance to the unit. It was Sam Western. 'The back door was open,' he said. 'I know the surgery is closed on Sundays, but I thought I'd just look in on Boris.'

'Come in, Mr Western,' Mrs Hope said warmly.

Sam Western came over to Boris's cage. 'How is he doing?'

'He's a bit sore and still groggy from the medication, but he's going to be fine,' said Mrs Hope. 'Luckily the pellets didn't do too much damage.'

'Ah, well. He's a strong healthy dog,' Sam Western said proudly.

'And bad-tempered and very noisy . . .' James whispered so that only Mandy could hear. Mandy's lips twitched.

Boris roused as he heard his owner's voice. Lifting his head, he gave a sleepy bark.

Mrs Hope opened the cage so that Sam Western could stroke Boris.

'Good lad,' Sam Western said fondly, scratching Boris behind the ears. Boris opened his jaws to give his owner a fierce doggy grin.

'Look at those teeth!' James muttered to Mandy.

Mandy nodded. 'I wouldn't give much for anyone else's chances of stroking Boris!' She waited until Boris's cage was locked once again, then said, 'Is there any news about the poachers, Mr Western?'

'Not so far, but I've told the police about the cartridges you found, and the tyre tracks,' Sam Western answered. 'It seems that there have been a few incidents round here during the past few weeks.'

'Do you think it's an organised set-up?' asked Mrs Hope.

'It could be,' replied Sam Western. 'The police seem to think so too. They're making enquiries, but these people are always hard to catch.'

'So, what about the deer?' Mandy said, unable to stop herself from speaking out. 'Are they still in danger?'

Sam Western gave her a hard look. 'You can be sure that I'm taking steps to protect my property. Dennis is organising security patrols during the night.'

Mandy knew that she could never think of the deer as property, but she was glad about the night patrols. Honey-Mum and Sprite would at least have some protection.

'That's a wise precaution,' agreed Mrs Hope. 'Poaching is a nasty business.'

Sam Western nodded shortly. 'It's not just the killing and stealing. Poachers aren't fussy about injuring animals. They damage a lot of stock, and I've spent good time and money managing the herd.'

Mandy opened her mouth, but at a look from her mum shut it again.

'Well, let's hope the police find the culprits before they do any more harm,' Mrs Hope said firmly.

'I can't argue with that,' Sam Western answered. 'Now, when can I take Boris home?'

'Oh, he'll be fine in a couple of days,' said Emily

Hope. 'Either myself or Adam will give you a ring to tell you when he can be collected.'

'Well, thanks,' Sam Western nodded and left to go about his business.

Mandy gave an explosive sigh. 'All that horrible man cares about is how much money he's going to lose because of poachers!' she said angrily. 'He doesn't care about animals at all!'

'Calm down, Mandy,' her mother said. 'Sam Western's a hard-headed sort, I grant you. But he did agree to leave the ancient woodland alone when he bought the wood, remember? And that meant he safeguarded the deer's home.'

'I suppose so,' Mandy said reluctantly.

'And you can't deny that he's fond of Boris.' Emily Hope put her arm round her daughter's shoulder and gave her a quick hug. 'Things are never simply black and white in this world,' she said.

'They are for Echo!' joked James.

'Oh, ha ha! Trust you, James Hunter!' Mandy said.

'Very good, James.' Mrs Hope chuckled. 'Now, who's for a nice cup of tea? There's some of your grandma's cake to go with it.'

'Great!' said James.

Mandy grinned as they all headed for the kitchen. James loved her gran's cooking.

Adam Hope arrived back from choir practice just as the kettle boiled. He looked at the rich fruitcake and plate of sticky flapjacks and rubbed his hands together. 'Lovely. Just the job!' he said, pouring a cup of tea.

Mandy couldn't wait to fill her dad in on all the details about finding Echo in the barn. And then there was Sam Western's visit. Between sips of tea, and helped by James, she told him everything.

'Well, you have been busy,' said Mr Hope, when Mandy and James had finished. He turned to his wife. 'It sounds like it hasn't been a very relaxing Sunday for you.'

Emily Hope shrugged. 'It couldn't be helped. But I was hoping to get some paperwork done before that vet's conference next week.'

Mandy swallowed a last mouthful of flapjack and jumped to her feet. 'Why don't James and I do the feeding in the unit this evening? Then you can do your paperwork. We don't mind, do we, James?'

James shook his head. 'No problem.'

Mrs Hope pushed back a stray red curl. 'Thanks, you two. That would be a great help.'

Mandy led the way to the feed cupboard in the unit. Inside, the shelves were stocked with tins and packets of every description. There was cat food, dog food, rabbit food, bird seed and food for animals on special diets.

'OK,' Mandy said, getting organised. She took down some tins of cat and dog food and a bag of rabbit food, then stacked them all on the food preparation counter at one side of the unit.

'I'll get some dishes down,' said James. He reached up to a shelf above the counter. As he took them down, the pile of clean metal bowls slid sideways. 'Whoops!'

James tried his best to catch them. Too late. They crashed to the ground with a tremendous noise.

Boris shot to his feet and began barking loudly. The kitten howled, her fur standing on end.

'Oh, no,' James said sheepishly. The noise was dreadful.

Mandy grinned. 'Never mind,' she called out. 'They'll settle down again in a minute.'

As she bent down to help pick up the bowls, her gaze fell on Echo's cage. Echo was awake, but still curled up on her blanket. She stared out placidly, her deep-brown eyes calm and untroubled.

'That's odd,' Mandy said, frowning. 'I thought Julia said Echo was jumpy.'

'She did.' James stacked the metal bowls on the counter.

'So how come Echo was so calm when those bowls crashed down and with Boris and the kitten making so much noise?' Mandy demanded.

James looked bemused. 'I don't know. It's weird, isn't it?'

Mandy fell silent, trying to puzzle it out. Then everything started to come clear. 'Unless . . . That's it! James! I think I might know what's wrong with Echo!'

Five

As soon as all the animals in the unit had been fed, Mandy hurried back into the cottage. James followed her into the study.

'Mum!' Mandy burst out excitedly. 'I think I know why Echo's so nervous. She can't help it. I think she's deaf – just like Maisy!'

Maisy was a beautiful Dalmatian with liver brown spots and amber eyes. She belonged to Elise Knight, who was a writer.

Emily Hope was sitting at Grandad's big old desk. She looked up from her notes with a patient smile. 'What's all this about Echo and Maisy?' she asked.

Mandy began again, more slowly this time. 'We were feeding the animals and James dropped a whole stack of dishes.'

'It made a terrific noise,' added James, blushing bright red. 'Boris went wild.'

'The other animals nearly jumped out of their skins too,' Mandy went on. 'Except for Echo!'

'And Julia already said that Echo won't come when she calls her,' James reminded Mrs Hope.

'So you put two and two together?' Mrs Hope said with a smile.

'Yes! And then we thought about Maisy!' Mandy said. It all seemed so clear now. 'Remember how Elise was worried because Maisy wasn't as lively and alert as she should have been for her age?'

'That's right,' said her mum. 'I ran some tests and found out that Maisy was deaf.'

'So you could run the same tests on Echo, couldn't you?' Mandy said. 'Then we'd know if my hunch was right.'

Mrs Hope nodded slowly. 'I've a feeling you could be on to something. I'll have a word with Julia and her parents when they call in tomorrow.'

'Couldn't you just take a quick look at her now?' Mandy pleaded. 'It wouldn't take long.'

Mrs Hope gave a long sigh. Then she stood up.

'Come on, then. I expect this paperwork can wait for another few minutes.'

'Thanks, Mum,' Mandy said, giving her a hug. 'You're a star!'

In the unit, Mandy opened Echo's cage. She reached in and gently scratched the top of Echo's head. She could still feel the slight lump there.

'Don't worry, Echo,' Mandy whispered. 'Mum is going to find out what's wrong with you.'

Echo looked alert and her tail wagged eagerly. But as soon as Mandy stopped looking directly at her, she seemed to lose interest. She lay down again and stared into space.

'She's acting just like Maisy did before Mum found out what was wrong,' Mandy said to James.

'Poor Echo,' said James. 'No wonder she seems jumpy and nervous.'

Emily Hope stayed at the side of the room out of Echo's line of vision. She snapped her fingers and called Echo's name. But Echo didn't look round. She just lay in her cage, her nose on her paws.

When Mrs Hope came back round to the front of her cage, Echo looked up at her. Her tail wagged slightly.

'Well, she certainly could have a hearing problem, but I think she's still too weak to run proper tests,' Mrs Hope concluded. 'And without them it's going to be difficult to be sure.'

'Oh.' Mandy felt disappointed. It looked like they were going to have to wait a bit longer before finding out if her theory was right. 'Thanks for looking at Echo again anyway.'

'No problem.' Mandy's mum ruffled her daughter's fair hair. 'I know you and James are eager to get to the bottom of this. 'Now – I really have to catch up with those notes!' She went out of the unit.

James had to go too. Mandy went to see him out.

'When do you think your mum will do the tests?' James asked at the front door.

'Probably in a day or two,' Mandy guessed. 'Julia and her parents are calling in tomorrow to collect Echo. I suppose she'll have to ask them if it's OK.'

James nodded. 'I have to go and buy a new school uniform with Mum tomorrow morning.' He pulled a face at the thought. 'But I'll meet you later.'

Mandy grinned. James hated going shopping for clothes. But if it had been for a computer or a new camera lens, he wouldn't have minded at all!

'Hi there. Welcome to the usual Monday chaos!' Simon, the practice nurse, called as Mandy came in from the unit the following morning. 'How are our patients today?' Simon wanted to know.

Mandy smiled. 'Boris is even more grumpy and snappy, which must mean he's feeling better! And Echo seems a lot stronger.'

'That's good.' Simon's eyes twinkled in a friendly fashion behind his wire-rimmed glasses. 'Your dad's just been called out to one of the farms. A cow has slipped and hurt her leg, so your mum and I are holding the fort.'

'I can help out. I'm not meeting James till later,' Mandy said.

'You're a real life-saver,' Simon grinned as he called out for the next patient to come through. 'See you later,' he said to Mandy, as he disappeared into one of the treatment rooms.

'Phew!' Mandy said. 'Simon wasn't joking about the chaos!' There was a long queue at reception. Every chair was occupied by owners, some with pet carriers, others with dogs on leads.

'So you'd better make an appointment for a

week from today for a check-up. But that leg's doing fine.' Mandy's mum appeared at the door of the treatment room followed by Robbie Grimshaw and Biddy, his Welsh collie.

'Now, Reverend Hadcroft, if you'd like to bring Jemima in,' Emily Hope called to the next patient. She glanced round the packed waiting room and gave her daughter a grateful smile. 'Oh, good. I'm glad you're here to lend a hand, love.'

Mandy grinned. 'One down, fifty to go!' she joked as Reverend Hadcroft carried his cat in for treatment. She went across and slipped behind the reception desk. 'Who's next, please?' she asked politely.

Jean Knox, the grey-haired receptionist, flashed her a grateful glance. 'Thanks, Mandy. I've hardly had a moment to think since we opened. And I can't seem to find my glasses . . .' She plucked at her cardigan where her glasses usually hung on their chain.

Mandy hid a smile. Jean was really nice, but so absent-minded. 'They're on top of your head,' she whispered.

'Oh, thank you. Silly me.' Jean pulled her glasses on to her nose.

For the next half hour Mandy was kept busy

handing out prescriptions and dealing with cheques. The queue gradually became smaller.

Suddenly the front door burst open and a woman rushed in. She was carrying a fluffy grey cat wrapped in a blanket. 'Can I see someone right away?' she asked in a shaky voice. 'Penny's been hit by a car!'

Emily Hope had just finished with a patient. She stepped forward and beckoned to the woman. 'Bring her straight through,' she said. 'Mandy, I could do with an extra pair of hands, please.'

Mandy leaped into action and followed the distressed woman into the treatment room. She helped keep Penny calm while her mum examined her. Luckily there were no broken bones.

When the woman had been given some pills to reduce the swelling, Mandy went back into reception. Julia and her parents were just arriving for their appointment.

'Hello,' Julia said with a bright smile. Her dark hair was drawn back into a pony-tail and she was wearing jeans and a yellow T-shirt. 'We've come to take Echo home.'

'I'm sure that's OK,' Mandy said. 'But I think Mum wants to have a word with you about her before she goes home.'

Julia's dark brows shot together. 'Why? What's wrong?' she asked.

'Oh, no. Now what?' said Julia's father under his breath.

'Here's Mrs Hope now,' Julia's mum said soothingly. 'Come on, let's all go and listen to what she has to say.'

'You know something, don't you?' Julia said to Mandy, when they were all in the unit.

Mandy nodded and glanced at her mum.

Emily Hope smiled. 'Go ahead, Mandy. Tell Julia and her parents what you and James have found out.'

Once again Mandy repeated the story of the dropped metal dishes and Echo's lack of reaction. 'And we know a gorgeous Dalmatian called Maisy, who had symptoms a bit like Echo's,' Mandy went on. 'Mum did some tests and found out that Maisy was deaf. So, anyway, I thought that Echo might be deaf too, like Maisy and because of the dishes. And then . . .'

'Deaf? But that isn't possible!' Julia's father interrupted.

'No way! Echo can't be deaf,' Julia agreed. She faced Mandy with her hands on her hips.

'But . . .' Mandy was taken aback by Julia's

certainty. 'How can you know for sure?'

'Because she was tested for deafness when she was a puppy. She passed all her tests with flying colours!' Julia said triumphantly. 'And, anyway, Echo was really easy to train when we first had her.'

'That's right,' Mr Hampton confirmed. 'She had a lovely nature. That's why we chose her over other pups in the litter. It's only been recently that there's been any problem with her.'

'Was there no sign of hearing loss at all?' asked Emily Hope.

'No.' Julia shook her head, so that her pony-tail bobbed about.

'Oh.' Mandy fell silent. This just didn't make sense. She glanced at her mum and saw that she was frowning.

'Well, Echo's certainly posing us a puzzle,' said Mrs Hope. 'I really thought Mandy and James were right.'

So did we, Mandy thought glumly.

'Is it OK if we take Echo home now?' Julia asked eagerly.

Mrs Hope smiled. 'I don't see why not. She'll be fine after a bit more rest. But I'd make sure you keep her on a lead, until you can be certain that she will come when you call her.'

'Oh.' Julia looked disappointed. 'What a shame. Echo loves running. She's really going to miss being out on the dales with me.'

'That can't be helped for now,' said Julia's mum. 'We don't want a repeat of this latest incident, do we?'

Julia shook her head, looking miserable. Then she brightened up. 'Anyway, it's brilliant to have Echo back, isn't it?'

Mandy couldn't help noticing that there was a slight hesitation before Julia's parents smiled and nodded.

Julia and Echo's problems are not over yet, she thought sadly.

After Julia had left with Echo, Mandy went back into reception. It was almost time for surgery to close. She began tidying up. The door opened and a pretty young woman with a Dalmatian on a lead came in. It was Elise Knight with Maisy. Mandy smiled broadly. What a coincidence!

'Hello, Mandy. Am I too late?' asked Elise. 'I just popped in to pick up some worming tablets for Maisy.'

'Hi, Elise,' Mandy said delightedly. 'No, it's

OK. There's ten minutes before we close. Shall I get the tablets, Jean?' she offered.

'Oh, would you, dear? Thanks.' Jean looked up from her computer. 'Hello, Elise. Maisy looks well.'

'She is, thanks,' answered Elise, looking down proudly at her dog. She stroked Maisy's head. The Dalmatian looked up at her with alert golden-brown eyes.

'How's the training going?' Mandy asked as she handed Elise the small packet.

'Maisy's doing brilliantly. Far better than I'd expected.' Elise smiled broadly as she counted out the money for the worming tablets. 'I can even let her off the lead for a run now. As soon as I blow her special whistle, she comes back straight away.' It had been Mrs Hope's idea that Maisy might be able to hear a high-pitched dog whistle. Mandy knew that humans couldn't hear the whistle, but animals could.

'That's great!' Mandy said. She came round the desk to say hello to Maisy. Making sure she was in the dog's line of sight, she slapped her hands on her knees in an eager 'come here' sign. Maisy's beautiful eyes lit up and she bounded across the room.

'Whoa!' Mandy laughed, staggering backwards, as the Dalmatian jumped up at her. She rubbed her face against Maisy's head. 'Hello, gorgeous!'

Elise Knight laughed. 'That's one signal she has no problem with!' She touched Maisy's shoulder to get her attention. Then she pointed to the ground. 'That's enough fuss now. You'll push Mandy over!'

Maisy looked up at her owner, then sat down obediently.

'Clever girl.' Mandy patted and praised Maisy.

'You and James must take some of the credit,'

said Elise. 'I don't think I'd have managed so well without your help.'

'That's OK,' Mandy said, feeling a bit embarrassed as she always did when people thanked her. 'We loved helping.' She knew that James would agree. She glanced down at Maisy, who was lying down with her nose on her paws. Mandy was struck by the way Maisy stared into space when no one was talking directly to her, just like Echo did. 'We had a Dalmatian here last night called Echo,' she told Elise. 'We thought she might be deaf too, like Maisy. Only she had all the tests at birth and they all came back clear.'

'Hmm, that does sounds puzzling,' Elise said. 'But if anyone can figure a problem out, it's your mum and dad. They're terrific vets!'

Mandy returned her smile. Elise was right. Her mum and dad were the best!

'I hope you find out what's wrong with Echo. Let me know if there's anything I can do,' Elise added.

'Thanks,' Mandy said. 'I will.'

'It's time we left,' said Elise. 'You must want to lock up. And Maisy is looking forward to her walk.' She bent down and ran her hand halfway down Maisy's back. Gently but firmly, she pressed her fingers into the dog's backbone.

Maisy stood up instantly, her tail wagging madly. She turned her head and looked up at her owner. Elise took the dog's face in her hands to praise her. Then she made a walking movement with two fingers.

Maisy's tail wagged nineteen to the dozen. She whined eagerly.

'She certainly understood that,' Mandy said with a chuckle. 'You two are terrific.'

Elise smiled proudly. 'Maisy does all the hard work. She learns so quickly. I can't believe I was worried that I wouldn't cope at first. I don't know what I'd do without her now.'

'She is gorgeous.' Mandy bent down to give Maisy a hug, before Elise led her away. 'Bye,' she called. 'Take care!'

After surgery closed, she phoned James and arranged to meet him. She fetched her bike from the shed, then cycled down the lane. James was waiting for her at the Fox and Goose crossroads. 'How's Echo?' he asked straight away.

Mandy told him, then explained about Maisy and Elise calling into the surgery too. After she finished speaking, James looked puzzled. 'So there's no point in your mum doing those tests?'

'Doesn't seem like it,' Mandy said. 'Julia is certain that Echo can't be deaf.' She shrugged. 'It's still a mystery. Did you get your new uniform?'

James nodded. 'Everyone else was doing the same. It took ages . . .'

Mandy felt a laugh bubbling up at the disgusted look on his face.

'And now Mum's just remembered that she forgot to stock up with wild bird food,' James went on. 'Do you fancy cycling over to the pet shop in Walton?'

'Try and stop me!' Mandy said with a wide grin. She loved going to the pet shop.

They cycled along the narrow winding road across the moor. The recent winds had stripped many leaves from the trees. A wet carpet of red, yellow and russet lined the verges.

They propped up their bikes outside Piper's Pets in the main street. James bought two plastic bags of wild bird seed and a huge bag of peanuts. 'I'll get Blackie a treat too,' he said, picking up a bone-shaped dog biscuit.

On their way back through Welford, Mandy stopped off at James's house to say hello to Blackie. 'Hello, boy!' She patted his solid wriggling body as he came hurrying out to meet them. Blackie jumped up and licked her chin.

'Get down, Blackie!' James ordered, his face red. 'Push him off, Mandy. I'm trying to teach him not to jump up.' Blackie ignored James. He gave a short bark and pawed Mandy's jeans, asking for more fuss.

Mandy grinned. 'Blackie will get the idea – in about ten years' time! Never mind. He's still lovely!'

But she couldn't help but contrast the boisterous Labrador with poor nervous Echo. Something was definitely wrong with the Dalmatian. And there just had to be a way to find out what it was.

Six

A growl rumbled in Boris's throat as Mandy filled his water dish the following morning. His dark eyes glared out of his broad wrinkled face.

'And thank you to you too!' Mandy said dryly. Then she heard a chuckle behind her. She turned round and saw her father coming into the unit.

'You won't have to put up with this ungrateful patient much longer,' he said. 'He's well on the mend now. Time he went home.'

Mandy grinned. 'I reckon Boris likes everyone to think he's a hard case. But he's mad about me really!'

Adam Hope smiled. 'Sensible dog!' He ruffled

his daughter's hair. 'I'll go and phone Sam Western now. I have to make another call to High Cross Farm this morning. It's near Upper Welford Hall, so I can drop Boris off.'

'High Cross Farm? Is something else wrong with Lydia's goats?' Mandy was instantly concerned.

'No, nothing like that. I promised to take her a tin of vitamin powder, that's all. And a couple of other things . . .' Adam Hope tailed off.

I bet you're not charging her for them, Mandy thought. Her kind-hearted dad knew that Lydia Fawcett didn't have a lot of money. 'Can James and I get a lift with you?' she asked. 'We could stow our bikes on the roof rack and then go for a bike ride when we've dropped Boris off.'

'Sounds like you've got it all worked out,' observed her dad.

'I have!' Mandy said. 'We still want to get some photos for the competition. I'll phone James and tell him we'll pick him up!'

'Ah, that's right. You didn't manage to take many photos when you were last up at Glisterdale, did you?' remembered Adam Hope.

Mandy shook her head. 'We were too busy trying to find Echo, then poor old Boris was shot by the poachers.'

'Speaking of poachers, make sure you and James keep out of those woods,' Adam Hope warned.

'OK. We'll be careful,' Mandy promised. She felt the familiar sick feeling in her stomach at the thought of the poachers preying on the lovely fallow deer. She went to phone James, then came straight back.

'Right. All set?' Mr Hope rubbed his palms together. 'Shall we get our grumpy friend here into the Land-rover?'

'Grr-uff!' Boris blinked hopefully at them through the cage.

Mandy laughed. 'I think he knows he's going home!'

'Here we are.' Adam Hope drove the Land-rover through the big double gates. Gravel crunched beneath the tyres as they drew up in front of an imposing stone doorway with ivy around it.

Mandy glanced around. She had been to Upper Welford Hall a few times. The lawns were like green velvet, and every tree and bush was clipped into a precise shape. At the end of the lawn, there was an ornamental lake with Canada geese and weeping willows. 'It's all very nice,' she commented to James. 'But I'd rather have our own garden!'

James nodded in agreement. 'You wouldn't dare to walk on Mr Western's lawn in case you left a mark.'

Sam Western himself answered the front door. 'Ah, you've brought Boris back,' he said, looking pleased. He came round to the back of the Land-rover.

Adam Hope opened the boot and stood back to let Mr Western see his dog.

'Come on, old fellow.' Sam Western reached in and lifted Boris out. Boris whined, but didn't struggle. 'Can he walk?' Sam Western asked.

'Yes, but gently does it. No strenuous activity for a week or so.' Adam Hope watched as Sam Western placed his dog gently on the ground.

'Right you are. Thanks for dropping him off,' Sam Western said gruffly. 'Come on, Boris.'

Boris waddled awkwardly towards the open front door. Then he stopped and glanced over his shoulder. His round black eyes sought out Mandy and he gave a short bark, his crooked rosette of a tail wagging.

'Goodness! I think he just said thank you!' said James in amazement.

Mandy took a step forward, meaning to give Boris a farewell pat. But Boris growled and nipped into the house. Mandy laughed. At least Boris was consistent!

Sam Western stood in the doorway. 'I'll call by to settle the bill in a day or two,' he said, closing the door.

'It's usual to pay by cheque on collection of your pet . . .' Adam Hope started to say, but found he was talking to himself. The door had already closed.

'The cheek!' Mandy said, outraged.

Her father shrugged good-naturedly. 'There's one rule for Sam Western and one for everyone else. Oh, well. I know he'll settle sooner rather than later.'

Adam Hope drove away from Upper Welford Hall and headed for the high moors. The road twisted and turned as it became steeper. Mandy glimpsed the Beacon, which was a Celtic cross and a landmark for miles around. Welford lay spread out like a board-game in the valley below.

'Here you are, you two,' said Adam Hope, slowing down to a halt at the side of the road. Mandy and James got out. 'See you later!' They waved as the Land-rover turned into a stony track and headed for Lydia's farm.

'Race you!' Mandy flung herself on to her bike and set off at speed.

'You're on!' James hurtled after her.

Mandy bent forward over the handlebars as she sped down a long slope. Just as she was zooming past a drystone wall, James drew level with her. Mandy braked hard, then leaned against the wall, panting and laughing. 'I call that a draw!'

James took off his glasses and polished them on his sweater. He put them back on, then peered through the cleaned lenses. 'Hey! Is that who I think it is?'

Mandy looked across the fields. A doe and a well-grown fawn were nibbling bushes at the edge of the woods. She could just make out the fawn's blue ear tag. 'Honey-Mum and Sprite!' she gasped. 'Let's go over and say hello.'

They left their bikes and went slowly across the field on foot. Honey-Mum and Sprite lifted their heads, watching Mandy and James closely.

Just a bit nearer, Mandy thought. She took another step, then held out her hand. For a moment she thought the deer were going to turn away, then Sprite stepped forward on her long delicate legs.

She came right over and stopped in front of

Mandy. Sprite's velvety nose quivered and her ears swivelled. Mandy hardly dared move. Then Sprite reached her head forward.

Mandy felt a damp cold nose push at her hand. 'Oh, Sprite! You remember me,' she whispered delightedly.

'This is great,' murmured James. He fished in his shoulder-bag for his camera.

Mandy barely noticed what James was doing. 'You're so beautiful,' she breathed, stroking Sprite's graceful curved neck. She had a warm feeling in her chest. It was such a privilege to have a wild animal trust you.

Honey-Mum came forward and stood next to the fawn. She reached out her head and butted Mandy's arm. 'Do you want some fuss too?' Mandy murmured, stroking Honey-Mum's velvety ears.

In the background, Mandy could hear James clicking away with his camera. But she only had eyes for the deer. As James put his camera back in its case, he began stroking Honey-Mum and Sprite too.

Honey-Mum snuffled at James's hair. 'It feels funny!' he spluttered. 'All hot and tickly.'

Mandy laughed as James screwed up his face. Sprite began moving away, and Mandy gave her a final pat. 'Off you go, then.'

She and James stood and watched as Sprite and Honey-Mum wandered back to the bushes. Sprite's long legs carried her lightly through the grass. She stretched up her head and began nibbling at some oak leaves.

'Stay safe. And watch out for poachers,' Mandy whispered. She turned to James. 'Wasn't that wonderful?'

'The best,' he agreed as Sprite and Honey-Mum disappeared into the trees. 'Shall we go back to our bikes? I wouldn't mind riding round the edge of the wood.'

Mandy nodded. 'Fine by me.'

They jogged back across the field, then cycled down a track that led across the moors and came out near the woods. The sky was a clear bright blue against a row of yellow field maples.

'Hang on! Can we stop a minute?' James had spotted something he wanted to photograph. Mandy sat on her bike, watching James point his camera at a huge black crow sitting on a slab of limestone.

'Go it!' he said in triumph. 'I reckon that could be a winner!'

Mandy grinned. James said that every time he took a photo. They stopped twice more – once to photograph starlings massing around an oak tree, the other to snap a cheeky robin, picking grubs out of a drystone wall.

By now they had reached the road that circled the edge of Glisterdale forest. It was a warm day and Mandy was feeling hot. 'Let's stop for a drink by those trees,' she suggested, heading for a wide grass verge.

James was in front. Mandy saw him looking from side to side, still alert to anything that might be worth photographing. As he turned round to say something, a herd of deer broke cover and darted towards the road.

'Watch out!' she yelled.

James's head whipped back round. He braked hard and his bike slewed sideways in a shower of stones.

The deer leaped across the road only a metre or so in front of them. Their eyes were wide and panicked. More of them burst from the trees and dashed away across the open moor, scattering in all directions.

Mandy skidded to a halt.

'Phew! That was close,' James said shakily. 'Something must have scared them badly.'

'Yes!' Mandy's heart was beating fast. 'I didn't

see whether Sprite and Honey-Mum were with the herd. Did you?'

James shook his head and held up his hands. 'It happened so fast. But I think we'd have seen that blue ear tag.'

'Yes, of course,' Mandy agreed. She was grateful for James's cool logic, but she didn't know whether to feel worried or relieved.

Suddenly an explosion ripped through the air. High and sharp, it came rattling out of the trees. Gunfire! Mandy felt her stomach lurch. 'Poachers!' she said in a horrified whisper.

'Oh, no!' James's mouth dropped open.

Mandy's thoughts whirled. Visions of injured or dying deer crowded her head. There must be lots of other deer still in the forest, among them Sprite and Honey-Mum. What could they possibly do? Suddenly she knew. 'Come on!' She threw herself off her bike and dumped it on the grass.

'Shouldn't we tell someone?' James called.

But Mandy had made up her mind. 'In a minute. I've got to check that the deer are OK first.'

'Wait for me.' James's face was pale but determined. He threw his bike down next to Mandy's and entered the tangle of trees and bushes after her.

Mandy's heart was in her mouth as she crept forward and pushed the branches aside. The thick carpet of leaves rustled under her trainers. Loud shouts reached them. They could hear heavy boots crashing through the bracken. Suddenly, Mandy froze.

Through the trees, she could see a number of burly men grouped around a smart dark blue van. They all held guns. On the ground three deer lay unmoving in a pool of blood.

'Oh, no!' Mandy's stomach clenched in sadness and horror.

'Hurry up! Let's get these loaded,' one of the men ordered. He wore an expensive-looking dark green jacket and jeans tucked into wellingtons.

Mandy saw the deers' heads hanging limply as they were loaded into the van. Hot tears ran down her cheeks. This was so hateful, she could hardly bear it. Frantically, she searched for a fawn with a blue ear-tag. But Sprite wasn't among the fallen deer. Mandy squeezed her eyes tight shut in a moment of thanks. Sprite and Honey-Mum must have bolted deeper into the forest.

'Do you recognise any of the men?' James whispered in a shaky voice.

'No.' Mandy shook her head. She dashed away

her tears, a hard knot of anger building inside her. 'How dare they?' she hissed in outrage. 'They're shooting the deer in broad daylight!'

'They look pretty well organised, don't they? That bloke in the dark coat seems to be in charge,' said James. The man was talking to another man who had neat grey hair and a small moustache.

Mandy swallowed hard, trying to calm down enough to fix the men's faces in her memory.

'We can't help those deer now,' James said quietly. He pulled at Mandy's sleeve. 'Come on. We have to tell the police.'

James was right. Mandy took a final glance at the awful scene. The men had finished loading the deer. Mandy heard the slam of the van door closing. She noticed that the dark blue van had a deep scratch underneath the side window.

'Come on,' James urged again.

Mandy nodded, gulping back tears, and turned away to follow James. They edged back the way they had come, trying to make as little noise as possible. Ahead of Mandy, James had his head down, forging a way through the thick bushes.

Mandy spotted a flash of reddish brown through the trees off to one side. Oh, no. More deer were in danger! She turned, ready to go after the deer and shoo them away from the poachers. But there was no time.

Suddenly an explosion split the air behind her. Mandy jumped, her legs collapsing weakly under her.

'Run!' James yelled.

Mandy didn't need telling twice. She scrambled to her feet and hurtled through the trees. Brambles tangled in her hair and scratched her face, but she didn't stop.

More gunshots rang out, closer this time.

'Ow!' The noise resounded painfully in Mandy's ears. She stumbled and put her hands to her head.

James stopped and ran back to her. His eyes were wide and scared in his white face. Mandy saw his lips move, but she couldn't hear anything because of the loud ringing in her ears.

'Are – you – hurt?' James mouthed.

Mandy looked at him in confusion, feeling dazed and a bit sick. She shook her head to try and clear it. But her ears still rang.

James grabbed her arm and pulled her with him though the trees. Mandy stumbled along, trying to keep up, but her vision seemed blurred and her head throbbed and pounded as if someone was hammering at it from the inside.

Seven

On the ride home, Mandy clung grimly to her bike, moving her hands and feet mechanically. Her throat still ached with misery as she tried to put the horrible sight of the dead deer from her mind, but it seemed impossible.

James cycled along beside her, looking upset and worried. 'Are you still feeling dizzy? Do you want to stop?'

Mandy shook her head. His voice sounded all muffled. 'I just want to get home.'

It seemed to take for ever before they reached Welford. Mandy sighed with relief as they zoomed past the Fox and Goose crossroads and sped down the lane towards Animal Ark. James braked hard. He threw his bike down on the drive and helped Mandy dismount.

'Thanks. I'm feeling a bit better,' Mandy said. 'But my legs are wobbly.'

Emily Hope was in reception, speaking to Jean Knox. She took one look at Mandy and James, taking in their muddy jeans and strained faces. 'What's happened?' She came over and put her arm around Mandy.

'The poachers came back,' Mandy said, her voice sounding strange and hollow inside her head. Her eyes filled with tears. 'Oh, Mum. They shot some deer. It was awful. We saw them being loaded into a van.'

'We were leaving to get help when Mandy saw some more deer in danger,' said James.

'I was going to chase them away, but then there were some gunshots right near us,' Mandy said. 'It was so loud it hurt my ears.'

'Right.' Emily Hope looked grim as she took charge. She ushered them through to the kitchen where Mandy and James sank on to kitchen chairs. 'Don't move,' she ordered.

Mandy didn't think she could even if she wanted to. She felt utterly drained. James seemed to feel the same. He leaned forward in his chair, his hands hanging down between his knees.

Mandy watched as her mum picked up the phone and spoke to the police. 'Yes – in the woods, up near Upper Welford Hall. You will? Good. Thank you.' Mrs Hope looked serious as she replaced the phone. 'They're sending someone up there right away.'

'I hope they catch those monsters before they kill any more deer!' Mandy said in a choked voice. Then she glanced up at James. 'Do you think they shot the deer we saw when we were leaving?'

James shrugged miserably. 'Maybe. I don't know,' he murmured.

'I just hope they got away . . .' Mandy said, her voice trailing off.

Emily Hope came over and knelt on the floor by her daughter's chair. She smoothed Mandy's hair back from her face. 'It must have been really horrible for you and James.'

Mandy nodded: the pictures were fresh in her mind – the dark blue van, the hateful sound of the guns, the beautiful deer lying dead. 'What sort of people are they?' she burst out angrily. 'Haven't they got any feelings?'

Her mum patted her arm. 'I expect they are

more concerned with the money they'll make. It's hard to believe people can be so callous, isn't it? Luckily there are far more people in the world who care about animals.'

Mandy nodded. She felt the anger starting to fade. Her mum always seemed to know just the right thing to say.

'How do your ears feel now, love?'

'A bit strange,' Mandy admitted. 'I've still got ringing in my ears and everything sounds really weird. Am I going to be deaf now?' she asked worriedly. If this was how Echo felt, then no wonder she was timid and edgy all the time.

'Don't be silly!' Emily Hope laughed. 'The ringing will soon fade.'

'I feel a bit dizzy too,' Mandy said.

'Your balance is affected,' said her mum. 'That's normal with ear problems. It won't last long.' She looked at James and smiled. 'At least you seem to be in one piece.'

'I was in front of Mandy, so I was further away when we heard the gunshots,' said James.

'I almost fell over, but James grabbed me and pulled me on,' Mandy said.

'That was brave of you.' Emily Hope gave James a warm smile.

James blushed bright red. 'Anyone would have done it.'

'I'm not sure they would.' Mrs Hope pushed back a strand of her red hair. 'Now, I'd better wash these scratches on your face and hands, Mandy.'

Adam Hope came in to the kitchen as Emily Hope finished putting cream on Mandy's scratches. James was washing his muddy hands at the kitchen sink. 'Looks like someone's been in the wars,' said Mr Hope, looking concerned. 'What's been going on?'

Emily Hope lifted one eyebrow and gave Mandy and James a cool look. 'These two almost had a run in with the poachers. There was some shooting and Mandy was rather too close to the gunfire for comfort. The loud bangs hurt her ears.'

'What! You've been hurt?' Adam Hope looked alarmed.

Mandy had been staring glumly at the table. Now she spoke up hastily. 'It's OK, Dad. I'm fine . . .' She tailed off at the look on her dad's face.

'Well, thank goodness for that, Mandy!' her father said in an exasperated voice. 'Didn't you think of the danger?'

'Of course not,' Emily Hope answered for her daughter. 'She couldn't think of anything but the deer. Animals always come first with you, don't they, Mandy?'

Mandy bit her lip, but didn't reply. She was starting to feel guilty about worrying her mum and dad.

'I suppose you've informed the police?' Adam Hope said to his wife.

Emily Hope nodded. 'They're sending someone straight up there.'

'Oh, well. I suppose there's no real harm done,' Mr Hope said after a long pause. 'Although it looks like you two have had quite a fright.'

'We did,' Mandy and James agreed.

'So perhaps we'll say no more about this – this time,' Emily Hope decided in her clear sensible way. 'But will you promise me that you'll count to ten before rushing in next time?'

'I'll try,' Mandy promised.

'And pigs might fly,' James whispered, so that only she could hear.

Mandy dug him in the ribs. She knew that she'd been let off lightly.

'Yes, no more heroics, you two,' Adam Hope said firmly. 'Let the police take care of the poachers.'

'OK,' Mandy and James said together.

Mandy's father let out a long sigh. 'I don't know about anyone else, but I need a cup of tea.' He filled a kettle and put tea bags into mugs.

Mandy started to get up. The room seemed to tip and she swayed. It really was a strange sensation. 'Uh-oh!' She sat down again quickly.

Suddenly she thought of something. She turned to her mum and dad, her heart beating faster with excitement. 'Wait a minute! Could Echo have been deafened by gunshots? Julia said that Echo loves running in the woods by Upper Welford Hall.'

'It's a possibility,' said Mrs Hope cautiously. 'But I think any deafness from gunshots would only be temporary. Thanks, Adam.' She took the mug of tea her husband handed her.

'Oh.' Mandy frowned, unwilling to let go of her theory just yet. There was something else niggling at the back of her mind. What was it? Then she had it. 'Echo's got that sore lump on her head, hasn't she, Mum? You said you thought it was an older injury.'

Emily Hope listened closely and nodded. 'Yes. There seemed no obvious explanation for it, but it seemed to have healed over.'

Mandy warmed to her idea. 'If Echo was nearby when the guns went off, she'd have been terrified, wouldn't she? Maybe she bolted and hit her head on a tree or something. Could *that* make her deaf, do you think?'

'I suppose so,' agreed her mum, looking thoughtful. 'But it would be very unusual. It might be an idea to find out when Echo started behaving badly, and if Julia noticed the lump on her head around that time.'

'We could phone Julia. She might know something,' suggested James.

'Great idea,' Mandy said. 'I'll go and do it now.'

'I think you'll have a problem with that,' said Adam Hope.

'Why?' Mandy asked.

'Ever tried having a phone conversation with your ears ringing?' her dad teased gently.

'No problem,' Mandy said, undaunted. 'James can phone Julia. He can tell me what she says.'

'Fine by me,' said James.

'There's no stopping you, is there, Mandy Hope?' Emily Hope shook her head, smiling.

'Nope!' Mandy said. 'Come on, James. We'll use the phone in the hall.'

Julia Hampton answered the phone on the third ring.

'Hi, Julia,' said James. 'Mandy and I wanted to have a word with you about Echo. Is that OK?'

At Julia's answer, James gave Mandy a thumbs-up sign.

Mandy listened as James explained their idea about the gunshots and Echo hitting her head.

'Ask her if she heard anyone shooting up at the woods when she was taking Echo for a walk recently,' Mandy prompted.

James relayed Mandy's question. 'She says yes, she did,' he said, when Julia had finished speaking.

'When was that?' Mandy asked.

'Two weeks ago,' came the answer.

Mandy frowned. 'I think that ties in with what Mr Western said. He told us there had been signs of poachers around the area for a couple of weeks. Can you ask Julia if Echo's behaviour got worse in the last two weeks or so?'

James repeated to Julia what Mandy had said. He listened to Julia speaking for a few seconds, then he turned back to Mandy. 'Julia thinks we're on to something. She says Echo's behaviour has definitely got worse since she heard the gunshots!'

'Tell her to hang on a minute. I'll go and tell Mum and Dad,' Mandy said. She went into the kitchen to give them the news. 'Julia thinks we're right about Echo! Everything adds up. What should we do now?'

'Well, I'd still like to do some proper hearing tests on Echo before we jump to conclusions,' said Mrs Hope. 'Tell Julia she can bring Echo in tomorrow if her parents agree.'

'Sure thing!' Mandy hurried back to James.

James relayed Mandy's question. Julia checked with her parents, then told James that her mum and dad had agreed to bring Echo in to Animal Ark for more tests.

'OK. Bye. See you.' James put the phone down.

Mandy looked at him with eager shining eyes. 'Julia's going to be so relieved when she finds out that Echo's not just being difficult!'

'Maybe.' James didn't look convinced.

'What do you mean?' Mandy asked.

'Think about it,' James said logically. 'Julia's parents are fed up with Echo's behaviour. She's become such a problem that they want to find her a new home. So how do you think they are going to react when they find out Echo's deaf?'

Mandy's heart sank. She saw at once what James was getting at. She had thought that finding out what was wrong with Echo would solve everything. But it might actually stir up a whole lot of new problems for Julia and her parents.

Echo stayed on Mandy's mind all afternoon. And there were the poachers to worry about too. Had the police arrested the gang responsible yet? Were Honey-Mum and Sprite still in danger?

She felt restless and uneasy. The ringing in her ears didn't help her mood. Her mum had suggested she spend a few hours relaxing with a book.

'Poor you,' said Adam Hope, when he found her curled up on the red sofa in the sitting room. A log fire crackled in the hearth, making the room warm and cosy. Mandy's dad had one arm behind his back. 'How's the temporary invalid?' he asked, his eyes twinkling.

'Bored, bored, bored.' Mandy managed a glum smile. 'Mum said to leave my chores until later. I can't hear the TV properly, I've finished all my homework, and I don't fancy reading.'

'Not even these!' Adam whipped a hand from behind his back to reveal two glossy magazines.

Mandy's eyes widened at the sight of the front covers with their pictures of exotic monkeys and birds of paradise. 'Oh, wow! Brilliant! These are great.'

Adam Hope grinned. 'I thought we could do with some new reading matter for the waiting room. The old magazines are falling to bits, so I took a quick trip to McFarlane's.'

Mandy grinned at her dad. He didn't fool her one bit – he had bought them to cheer her up. She threw her arms round him and gave him a hug. 'Thanks, Dad!'

'No problem, love. I'll see you later. I'm on duty in the surgery now.' He pulled a face. 'Mrs

Ponsonby is coming in. Pandora is due for a booster injection.'

'Good luck then!' Mandy chuckled. Mrs Ponsonby was the bossiest woman in the village, but she doted on her spoilt Pekingese, Pandora, and her lively mongrel puppy, Toby.

Mandy settled back on the sofa with the magazines. She was so engrossed that the rest of the afternoon passed quickly. She checked the clock and, finding it was almost time for supper, she leaped to her feet.

'Hey!' She stopped dead. The ringing had stopped and she no longer felt dizzy.

She dashed off to find her mum and dad and tell them the news. But a shadow passed over her good mood as she thought about Echo's tests the next day. Poor Echo – it looked like her problem wasn't going to be so easily resolved.

Eight

First thing the following morning, Mandy pulled on her jumper as she flew down the stairs and almost collided with her mum as she came out of the kitchen.

'Hey! Where's the fire?' Emily Hope teased.

'Sorry, Mum!' Mandy apologised. 'But I can't stop thinking about what happened in the woods yesterday. Could you phone the police, please?'

Mrs Hope nodded. 'I'll do it right away. I'm as anxious as you are to know if those men have been caught.'

She went into the hall. Mandy waited impatiently as she heard her mum talking to the police.

When Mrs Hope came back into the kitchen, Mandy searched her face eagerly. 'What did they say?' she asked. 'Did they arrest the poachers?'

Emily Hope shook her head. 'I'm afraid not, love. They sent someone up there straight after I phoned yesterday. They found plenty of evidence of poaching, but there was no sign of anyone.'

Mandy's spirits sank. This was awful. Somehow she didn't think that the poachers had finished up at Glisterdale Forest. They could come back at any time, which meant that Honey-Mum's and Sprite's lives were still at risk.

'Try not to think about the poachers, love,' Mrs Hope went on gently. 'Worrying never solves anything.'

'I know,' Mandy replied, thinking that her mum was right, but that it was easier said than done.

Just then Adam Hope came in from the back garden. He went to the sink to wash his hands. 'I'll never know how we manage to fill so many rubbish bags. I must have put out at least a hundred of them for collection.'

'Oh, sure!' Mandy laughed. And to think her dad was always teasing her for exaggerating! 'Sick animals can't help using up lots of bedding and stuff, can they?' she said.

'No. It's all part of the job,' Mr Hope agreed cheerfully, as he dried his hands. 'And I used to think being a vet was glamorous!'

Mandy pulled a face. 'It is!' she said firmly. 'It's the best job in the world!'

'Now, how did I know that you'd say that?' Mr Hope grinned as he filled the kettle and switched it on. 'I'm ready for some tea and toast. Anyone want to join me?'

Mandy was thoughtful as she ate her toast. Only a few days left now before term started. She loved school and was looking forward to catching up with friends she hadn't seen over the holidays. After they finished eating, Mandy helped clear away the dishes, then she went to do her chores. It wasn't very exciting to clean out cages and mop floors, but she knew it was an important part of animal care.

Just as she was putting the cleaning things back in their cupboard, Adam Hope popped his head round the door. 'Julia and her parents are here,' he told her.

'Brilliant timing! Thanks, Dad.' Mandy followed him through into the waiting room.

She found Julia and her parents sitting anxiously in a row. 'Hi, Julia. Hi, Mr and Mrs Hampton,' Mandy said.

'Hello, Mandy,' said Mrs Hampton with a rather strained smile.

'How's Echo been?' Mandy asked Julia.

'About the same,' said Julia. 'We've been keeping her in, except for short runs in the back garden. I really miss taking her out for walks.'

'Your mum's just taken Echo to be examined,' Mr Hampton said to Mandy. 'We were really shocked when Julia told us about the gunshots and how they could have affected Echo.'

'It's awful, isn't it?' Mandy agreed sadly. 'It looks like poor Echo's been really unlucky.'

Julia nodded miserably, close to tears. 'It's just not fair! Echo passed all her hearing tests when she was little, but now she might have been made deaf anyway!' She looked down and began twisting her hands in her lap.

Mr Hampton put a hand on his daughter's shoulder. 'Echo's getting the best treatment now, love. We'll soon know how she is,' he said gently.

'That's right. I expect Mum's doing the tests now,' Mandy said reassuringly.

Julia's head came up. 'Will they hurt her?' she asked anxiously.

'Oh, no.' Mandy reassured the worried girl. 'Mum will look inside her ears to check for any physical damage first. Then she'll go through a special routine. Basically, she'll stand behind Echo and make different noises. She marks the findings on a chart and the results will show Echo's level of hearing.'

'It doesn't sound too frightening,' Julia said, seeming to relax a bit, but her friendly face still looked strained. Mandy guessed Julia had spent a sleepless night worrying about her pet.

'Thanks for explaining that, Mandy,' said Mrs Hampton.

'That's all right,' Mandy said, wishing there was more she could do.

Just then two more owners and their pets came into the waiting room. As the reception became busier and other patients arrived, Mandy went to help Jean Knox.

'Thanks, Mandy,' said the receptionist, looking up from her appointment book.

Adam Hope dealt with each patient in turn. He called to Mandy to ask for her help and she gave him a hand to keep a Jack Russell pup calm while he dressed the pup's cut paw.

'Thanks, love,' said Mandy's dad when the Jack Russell and his owner had left. 'Why don't you go back and sit with Julia now?'

'OK.' But Mandy had hardly sat down when her mum appeared at the door of the treatment room.

'Would you like to come in now?' Emily Hope called out.

Mandy followed Julia and her parents inside. Echo didn't look round when everyone trooped in. She stood gazing at the floor, her head drooping slightly.

Julia went straight across to her dog and gave her a hug. Echo jumped at first, but seemed to relax when she recognised her owner's smell and touch.

'How is she?' Julia asked worriedly, stroking Echo.

'It's as we thought, I'm afraid,' said Mrs Hope. 'Echo has gone deaf. We'll probably never be sure what happened to her. But I think Echo was running in the woods when someone fired a gun very close by. It would have hurt her ears and probably confused and terrified her. My guess is that she panicked and ran into a tree or maybe a rock. That would explain the lump on her head.'

'Deaf? You see, Dad! Mum! Echo can't help her bad behaviour.' Julia leaped to her dog's defence at once. 'Poor Echo! She's had a horrible shock. It's no wonder she's so frightened and confused.'

'What an awful thing to happen.' Mrs Hampton shook her head sadly. She reached out and stroked Echo. 'She used to be such a lovely-natured dog.'

'She still is!' Mandy burst out, going round to stand in front of Echo. She cupped the dog's face in her hands like she had seen Elise do to Maisy. 'You're gorgeous, aren't you?'

Julia watched closely as Echo wagged her tail and licked Mandy's chin. 'She didn't jump at all when you touched her just now,' she said with surprise.

'That's because I made sure she could see me first. Once she knew I was there and what I was doing, she felt OK,' Mandy explained. 'You try it.'

Julia copied Mandy's actions. This time Echo stood placidly while Julia petted her. Julia looked pleased. 'Good girl, Echo. Thanks, Mandy.'

Emily Hope turned to Julia's parents. 'Now that we know what Echo's problem is, we can discuss your options.'

'Options?' Julia's dad repeated. 'Well, I can't help feeling that we've got an even bigger problem now.'

'What do you mean?' Julia rounded on her dad, her smile fading.

'Think about it, love. This isn't what we expected at all when we bought the dog. How's Echo going to lead a normal life? For a start, she needs loads of exercise, but you can't let her run free any more.'

'Why not?' Julia protested, putting her arm protectively round Echo's neck.

'Because she can't hear you calling her back. I expect that's why she's run away twice already,' Julia's mum added. She looked towards Emily Hope as if for confirmation.

Mrs Hope nodded gravely. 'That's probably true,' she said.

'Oh.' Julia bit her lip. She seemed to be starting to see her mum and dad's point of view.

Mr Hampton spoke up. 'And what about the effect this has on Echo's temperament? I can see why she's been so nervous recently, but even though we know the reason it doesn't mean we can do anything about it. We're going to have to start all over again with her training.'

'I won't deny that it will take a lot of time and patience,' agreed Emily Hope.

Julia's eyes filled with tears. 'But I want to help Echo. I just don't know where to start.'

Mandy stroked Echo's smooth neck. Echo whined softly, then turned and licked her hand. 'Elise Knight felt like that at first,' Mandy said. She explained that Elise was a local writer and that Maisy was her deaf Dalmatian. 'Now Elise says she wouldn't be without Maisy. They get on brilliantly and you'd never know that Maisy couldn't hear,' she finished.

'But if Elise is a writer, she probably works from home,' Julia's dad pointed out. 'That means she can give her dog all the time she needs. Julia will be back at school in a few days.'

Julia turned to her parents eagerly. 'That doesn't matter! I'll take Echo out early every morning. And I'll have evenings and weekends too. I know I can cope, especially if you'll both help me . . .'

Julia's mum shook her head slowly. 'Julia, love,' she said reasonably, 'I really think this is beyond us. We have to face facts.'

Julia looked at each of her parents in turn. 'So what are you saying? That we aren't even going to try?'

Mandy couldn't stay silent. 'But there's loads you can do for Echo! There are special dog whistles. And you can train dogs to respond to hand signals. James and I could help Julia, just like we helped Elise with Maisy . . .'

'That's enough, Mandy,' her mum said firmly. 'I know you want to help. But let's keep the suggestions back until everyone's thought about this.'

Mandy knew her mum was right. But was there nothing anyone could say to persuade the Hamptons to keep Echo? She looked desperately at Julia. Surely she wanted to do everything possible for Echo?

Julia seemed to be finding the whole thing too much to bear. She gave a little sound of distress and buried her head in Echo's neck. 'There has to be a way, Echo. I won't give up,' she murmured tearfully.

Mrs Hampton patted her daughter's shoulder. 'I'm sorry, love. But I really think it would be better if we ask the Hopes if they can find a new home for Echo as soon as possible,' she said gently.

Emily Hope waited for a moment, then she nodded. 'I'll do my best, if that's what you want.'

'It isn't what we want, but I can't see any other way,' said Mr Hampton heavily.

'I understand,' said Mrs Hope. 'It's a difficult situation for you all.'

'Thank you so much for everything you've done for Echo,' Mrs Hampton added. She gave Echo a stroke. 'Poor girl,' she said softly.

Mandy's heart sank. Echo was so lovely. Surely she deserved a chance to stay with her owners? She cast a pleading look at her mother. 'Isn't there some other way . . .'

Emily Hope held up her hand. 'Hang on, Mandy. This has to be Julia's and her parents' decision.'

Julia raised a tear-stained face. 'Does . . . does Echo have to stay here?' she asked.

'No. We'll take her home,' Julia's dad said kindly. 'But only until a new owner can be found.'

Mandy had a lump in her throat as she watched Julia stand in front of Echo and look into her eyes. Then she took hold of the lead and tugged it gently. 'Come on, girl,' said Julia, tapping Echo on her shoulder. Echo's head came up, her tail wagged, and she trotted out obediently.

'Julia's a natural,' Mandy thought. She was sure that with a little help, Julia would be able to re-train Echo. But it looked as if she wasn't going to get the chance.

'Time for a break,' announced Emily Hope, when Julia and Echo had gone. 'And that's an order!'

Mandy trudged glumly through to the kitchen after her mum. She sat in a kitchen chair and propped her chin on her hand while Emily Hope made them both hot chocolate and piled biscuits on a plate.

'Cheer up, love,' she said. 'If you're going to be a vet, you'll need to learn that there's a point where you have to hang back and not get involved.'

'I know,' Mandy said. 'But sometimes it's really hard.' She sipped her chocolate. 'You know, Mum, Glisterdale Forest is lovely, but it seems to bring nothing but bad luck at the moment.'

'How do you mean?' asked Mrs Hope.

'Well,' Mandy replied. 'First there's poor Echo, then there's the poachers who haven't been caught yet. They could even be killing more deer right now.' She let out a long sigh. 'I'd really like something good to happen for a change!'

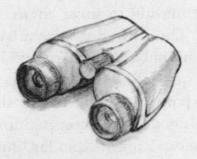

Nine

Mandy was in the recovery room when James arrived the following day. Her mum had been keeping an eye on Pippin, an old rabbit who had reacted badly to the anaesthetic. Mandy had popped in to check on him. 'How is he?' she asked.

'Pippin's coming round now. He'll be fine,' said Mrs Hope.

'That's good,' Mandy said, pushing open the door and going into the surgery. She saw James through the window. 'James's here, Mum! I'll see you later.'

'OK. Bye,' Emily Hope called after her.

James had brought Blackie with him and he had

binoculars and a camera slung over his shoulder. Mandy went outside to meet them. 'Hi, James. Hi, Blackie.' The Labrador gave a friendly woof and wagged his tail as Mandy patted his head.

'I thought we could take Blackie up to the dales for a walk,' James suggested. 'We still need to take some photos for the competition. I've only got those ones of . . . er . . . so far,' he faltered.

'Of what?' Mandy asked, puzzled.

'Nothing. Doesn't matter,' said James quickly.

Mandy shrugged. A walk was fine by her. It might take her mind off poor Echo. 'OK,' she said. 'But I don't think we'll see much wildlife if we have Blackie with us!'

James pretended to be hurt. 'I can always call him to heel. He's doing really well at dog training classes. Watch this. He's been learning to lie down on command.'

Mandy watched as James gave a gentle tug on the lead. 'Down,' he said firmly.

Blackie's ears pricked up. He gave a short bark, then jumped up and put his paws on James's chest.

'Oh, very impressive!' Mandy laughed as Blackie licked James's chin.

'Get off, Blackie!' James blushed and wiped his chin. 'OK, so he's still got some learning to do.'

'You can say that again! Never mind. Blackie's lovely just the way he is.' Mandy stroked the Labrador's soft ears. 'You wait here. I'll just pop back into the house and change into my boots.'

Adam Hope was in the kitchen. His white vet's coat was covered in muddy marks. 'Wet sheepdog with a gum infection – and a bad temper,' he explained with a grin as he stripped off the soiled coat.

Mandy reached into a cupboard for her

wellingtons. 'Are its teeth OK now?' she asked.

Her dad nodded. 'They will be once the antibiotic takes effect. But I don't know if this coat will recover!' Mandy laughed. Mr Hope tipped some washing powder into the slot, opened the door and bundled the coat in. He switched the machine on and looked towards the open back door where James waited with Blackie. 'Where are you two – or should I say three – off to?'

'We're taking Blackie for a walk to get some more photos,' Mandy told him. She had pulled on her boots and was zipping up her anorak.

'Good luck, then. See you later!' Adam Hope went out to get a clean white coat.

'Bye, Dad.'

'Bye, Mr Hope,' called James.

They went along the lane, where the hawthorn bushes were heavy with dark red berries. Mandy suggested they cut across the fields. It had rained hard in the night and the stubble was sodden underfoot.

'Heel,' James said hopefully as Blackie pulled at his lead. But Blackie took no notice. His nose was twitching at all the delicious scents.

Mandy soon felt her head beginning to clear as they climbed higher in the fresh autumn air.

'I'll let Blackie off now. We're miles from the road,' said James, unclipping the lead. Blackie trotted off to sniff out tracks in the grass.

Mandy and James splashed through the puddles. They kept an eye open for anything worth photographing. Birds circled high overhead, tiny black dots against the grey sky.

Mandy borrowed James's binoculars. 'Look! There's a squirrel in that tree!' She passed them over to James.

James peered at the squirrel. 'Nice. But it's a bit far away for a good photo.'

'What about those rabbits on top of that hill?' Mandy said.

Suddenly Blackie barked and shot forward. He'd seen the rabbits too. The Labrador laid back his ears and bounded across the field.

'Uh-oh!' Mandy said. She knew that Blackie had a one-track mind once he'd glimpsed the white bobtail of a rabbit.

'We'd better go after him!' James gasped.

Mandy and James stumbled up the long steep slope, the mud sticking to their wellies. By the time she reached the crest of the hill, Mandy was breathing hard. She looked out over the wide sweep of the dales. 'He's nowhere in sight,' she said.

James paused at her side. 'He could be anywhere.' He lifted the binoculars and scanned the slabs of limestone rock and open moorland that stretched into the distance.

Then Mandy glimpsed a dark shape between some trees in the valley bottom. 'He's down there! Come on,' she said, setting off again.

It was easier running downhill, but the wet grass was slippery. Mandy and James skidded to a halt in front of some birch trees just as Blackie came lolloping towards them. His tongue was hanging out and his breath steamed as he gave them a doggy grin.

'Where have you been?' James scolded. He made a grab for Blackie's collar, but it was too late. The Labrador turned tail and shot off through the trees.

Mandy groaned. 'Here we go again!'

'I'll never get any photos at this rate!' James complained.

Mandy thought it best not to remind him that it had been his idea to bring Blackie. They plunged into the trees after the black Labrador. It soon became even more soggy underfoot. Mandy saw water glinting through the birches. 'What's that splashing noise?' she began.

James rolled his eyes. 'Oh, no,' he groaned. 'He wouldn't . . .'

They emerged into a small clearing. The ground sloped down on all sides and a large pool of rainwater had gathered in the bottom. Blackie was rolling over and over in the leafy mud at the edge of the water. He seemed to be thoroughly enjoying himself.

'Blackie, stop that! Come here!' James yelled.

The Labrador stood up. His nose was wet and his thick black fur stuck up in muddy spikes. Mandy couldn't help laughing.

'Oh, that's just great. Mum will go mad!' James's face was red and annoyed. 'I'll have to bath him when we get home.'

'Don't worry. I'll help,' Mandy promised. 'We can clean him up at Animal Ark, if you like.'

James brightened. 'Thanks.' Then he began to laugh too. 'Blackie, you idiot! Look at the state of you!'

'There might not be a Dalmatian in the dales any more,' Mandy said. But there's definitely a mutt in the mud!'

Blackie blinked happily at them, his eyelashes spiky as well. His tail wagged merrily.

Suddenly, Mandy stiffened. On the far side of

the glade, a group of deer were stepping out of the trees. They were fallow deer – mostly does and fawns, but there was a buck with them too.

'Don't make any sudden movements,' Mandy whispered urgently.

'What?' James turned his head very slowly and drew in his breath. 'Oh wow! I must get my camera.'

The deer bent their slender copper-coloured necks and began drinking. The buck kept watch. His proud head was crowned with impressive spreading antlers. Mandy looked through James's binoculars. 'He's starting to shed the velvet on his antlers, can you see?' she asked.

'Yes. Isn't it brilliant?' James whispered back as he clicked away excitedly.

Mandy caught hold of Blackie's collar and patted his wet head. Blackie was still panting hard and seemed content to lay down, so Mandy was able to study the buck in peace. She knew that the velvet was a special sort of skin that covered the antlers until they were fully grown. 'It's amazing that the bucks grow a completely new set of antlers every year, isn't it?' she said. 'And every year they get more points on the antlers' branches. You can tell their age by how many there are.' She counted the points. 'This one's six years old.'

'Mmm.' James was engrossed in peering through the viewfinder. After a couple of minutes, the camera whirred loudly as it rewound the film. 'That's it! I've used up all the film.'

Just in time, Mandy thought. The deer were looking over at them nervously. Suddenly the buck gave a coughing bark and they all melted back into the trees.

'That was brilliant!' James enthused.

'Success at last! And it's all down to Blackie finding this pool for us,' Mandy said. She would have given Blackie a hug if he hadn't been so muddy.

James stowed his camera away in its case. 'I suppose we ought to make our way back to Animal Ark. It's going to take ages to get Blackie cleaned up.'

'Fine by me,' Mandy agreed. 'Shall we go up to the road and go home the easy way?'

'Good idea,' said James. 'That way, Blackie's not likely to want to go chasing rabbits again.'

'Or take another mud bath!' Mandy added with a chuckle. 'Although I don't think he could get any messier if he tried!'

They climbed up the slope and out of the clearing. As they made their way over the rough moorland on their way up to the road, a thin rain began to fall. Mandy shivered as grey clouds drifted in lower over the rolling hills, glad that they were going home. She thought longingly of the cosy kitchen and mugs of hot chocolate.

As they reached the road, James clipped on Blackie's lead and they started walking back towards Welford. Just then a dark blue van came speeding along the road towards them. It zoomed by and disappeared around a bend. Mandy felt a clutching sensation in her chest. It was the poachers' van!

'James! Did you see that?' she gasped.

James stood stock still. He nodded. 'It was heading for the woods!'

'You know what that means. More deer will be killed!' Mandy said furiously. Before she could think better of it, she turned and sprinted after the van. 'Come on,' she called over her shoulder. 'We have to do something!'

James ran after Mandy, Blackie loping along at his side.

Mandy's long legs carried her swiftly up the roads to the woods. She saw a car park ahead and dashed into it. She panted to a halt, looking left and right. No sign of the blue van. Then she spotted a forestry track, leading deeper into the trees. 'Over here!' she called to James. 'That track must be how they get to the deer!' She began heading after them.

James caught up with her. 'Hang on a minute. What's the plan?'

'I'll try and think of a way to distract the poachers,' Mandy puffed, thinking fast. 'Or maybe I can find the deer and chase them away out of danger. You run for help. Upper Welford Hall's on the other side of the forest. It'll be quicker to go there than run all the way back to the village!'

'I'm not leaving you on your own,' James protested.

Mandy hadn't got time to argue. 'I'll be OK. Just go!'

James seemed torn. Mandy thought he was going to insist on staying. Then he made up his mind. He thrust Blackie's lead into her hands. 'All right. I'll be as quick as I can. But I'm leaving Blackie with you!'

Mandy watched James speed away down the track. Her heart was thudding painfully. She set off again, praying that Blackie would behave himself for once. She felt desperate as she crashed through the trees. She just knew that she had to do anything possible to save even one more deer from being killed.

Branches whipped past her face as she kept alert for any movement. Suddenly she glimpsed the honey-gold coats of a group of young does. She took a deep breath and ran straight at the deer. 'Come on, Blackie!' she urged.

Luckily the Labrador seemed to understand what she wanted. He leaped forward, matching her pace.

Mandy waved her arms and shouted. 'Run away. Shoo! Go on. Run!'

From the corner of her eye, she glimpsed a part of the fence that ringed the woods. If she could just get the deer to jump it, they would be safe on the open moor. The startled does had retreated further back into the trees, but they paused a few metres away. Looking back at Mandy, they blinked curiously.

'Oh, no,' she groaned. Normally she would have been delighted that the does seemed interested in her. She would have loved to gain their trust. But now she had to try to scare them for their own good.

She ran towards them again, her arms waving like windmills. 'Go on! What are you waiting for?' she shouted desperately. 'Run!'

It was no use. The deer didn't move. Mandy almost sobbed with frustration. They would be easy targets if they stayed here.

Then Blackie surged forward again, almost pulling the lead from her hand. He gave a series of loud barks. The doe at the head of the group made a sharp little coughing noise. She stamped her feet and raised her tail to show the white fur underneath.

'That's it, Blackie. Good boy! Keep barking!' Mandy encouraged.

She watched as the doe warned the others of danger. Then they all turned tail and hurtled towards the fence.

'Yes!' Mandy called out in triumph. She let out a long sigh, watching as they reached the fence and each one of them sailed over it to the open moor. This time she could be certain that the deer were safe.

Mandy fell to her knees and hugged Blackie – mud and all. 'Good boy!' she praised him again. 'We did it. We saved the deer!'

Blackie whined and licked her face.

As Mandy rose to her feet, a cold breeze swept damp autumn mist all round her and she felt a surge of satisfaction. The mist would make it even harder for the poachers to follow the deer.

Suddenly a large dark shape came looming out of the trees. The poachers' van! There was no time to run. It came roaring down the track and screeched to a halt right in front of her.

Ten

Mandy's mouth dried. Her legs felt as if they had turned to jelly.

The van doors opened and three tough-looking men got out. Mandy recognised two of them from the other day, including the one wearing the dark jacket who seemed to be in charge.

Blackie growled menacingly. 'Down, boy,' she said, grabbing his collar to stop him leaping towards the van. Mandy swallowed hard, shaking with fright. But her chin came up as she glared defiantly at the men. She gave a small tug on Blackie's lead, urging him to walk forward with her. As she walked past the men, they stood and watched her.

Despite her fear, Mandy had a warm feeling inside her, because she knew that she had beaten them. Whatever the men did now, they couldn't harm the deer she had chased away.

The poachers seemed unsure what to do about her. Then one of them started to come towards her. Blackie's hackles rose. He growled warningly and the man hesitated.

'The police are on their way!' Mandy burst out, praying that it was true. James should have reached Upper Welford Hall by now.

She saw the men glance uneasily at each other.

Then the leader allowed his frown to relax a fraction. 'She's bluffing,' he said. 'Let's get on with it.'

Mandy's confidence slipped away. They were still going to look for deer! There seemed nothing else she could do. She had scared away one small group of deer, but there would be others nearby. And Honey-Mum and Sprite might be with them.

The men were opening the van and reaching for their guns. Blackie surged forward again, barking loudly and pulling against his collar. Mandy almost lost her balance as she tried to hang on to him.

'What about the dog?' One of the men eyed Blackie warily.

'I'll deal with it,' said the leader. He stood there, the shiny steel barrel of his shotgun gleaming menacingly. The polished wooden butt rested under his arm. He took a step towards Mandy and began to raise the gun.

'Oh, no! No!' Mandy's blood ran cold. She curved an arm protectively around Blackie's thick neck and squeezed her eyes shut.

There was a screech of brakes. Mandy's eyes flew open as three vehicles appeared through the trees, two police vans and Sam Western's Land-rover. Mandy heard doors slam, then loud voices rang out.

'Put down the guns! You're all under arrest!'

Mandy recognised the voice of Sergeant Wilkins, the wildlife officer from the police headquarters at Walton. She saw that policemen were piling out of the vans. They surrounded the poachers and the men laid their guns down without protest.

It was all over. Mandy's legs gave way. She sank down beside Blackie and hugged him close. His gritty wet fur felt wonderful against her cheek.

James scrambled out of Mr Western's Land-rover and came tearing over. His eyes looked huge and scared behind his glasses. 'Are you OK?' he asked anxiously. 'I . . . I saw that man aim his gun . . .'

Mandy looked up and smiled weakly. She blinked back tears. 'We're both fine. Blackie was a brilliant guard dog.'

James bent down and gave his pet a hug. 'Well done, boy!'

'You must have run like mad to have got back so soon,' Mandy said.

'Not really. I got winded before I was halfway to Upper Welford Hall,' James admitted. 'I was trying to catch my breath, when Sam Western came along in his Land-rover. As soon as I told him what was going on, he called the police on his mobile.'

Mandy beamed at him. 'Well, I think you did great, James Hunter!'

James blushed, but looked delighted. 'What about you? Did you manage to chase the deer away?'

'Oh, yes,' Mandy said with deep satisfaction. 'A whole lot of them jumped the fence. You, me, and Blackie did it together. We saved the deer!'

James grinned from ear to ear. 'That's great,' he said.

'We haven't done anything!' one of the poachers was protesting angrily. 'You can check the guns. They haven't been fired.'

'Maybe not today,' James muttered under his breath.

'You can't arrest us without evidence!' said the leader.

Mandy and James looked at each other in dismay. Surely the men weren't going to be allowed to get away?

But Sam Western was marching over to the poachers' van. He opened the back door and peered inside. 'Have a look at this, sergeant,' he called out with grim satisfaction. 'I think you'll find all the evidence you'll need right here!'

Two policemen went over the van.

'Just as well they didn't scrub it out,' said Sam Western. 'It should be no problem to check for traces of deer.'

'Oh, I've no doubt about what we'll find,' Sergeant Wilkins agreed.

'I need to call my solicitor,' the leader of the poachers said coolly. The other men didn't say anything. They seemed to realise that it was useless to argue as the police led them away.

Sergeant Wilkins came over to Mandy. 'Hello there,' he said. 'Fighting on the side of the animals again, eh? Well done, you two. We've been after this gang for some time. You can be sure that they'll be out of action for quite a while!'

'Good!' Mandy said with feeling. 'That means no more deer will be killed.'

Sergeant Wilkins nodded. 'Right. It's a good thing the deer had you and James looking out for them.'

'They're all safe now. That's the main thing,' Mandy said. She was cold, muddy and she still felt a bit shaky, but she was utterly satisfied with how things had turned out.

Sam Western appeared at her shoulder. 'You look frozen, young lady,' he said in his curt way. 'There's a blanket in the Land-rover. Come on.

Get in and I'll give you and your friend a lift home.'

'Thanks, Mr Western. A lift would be great.' Mandy pushed a strand of damp blonde hair out of her face.

'Think nothing of it,' came the brusque reply. 'Besides, I'd like a word or two with your mum and dad.'

Mandy groaned inwardly as she climbed into the Land-rover. She was going to have some more explaining to do, especially as her parents had told her not to go back into the forest.

'You'd better put your dog in the back,' Sam Western said to James.

'Thanks.' James put the Labrador in the back behind the dog screen, then he got in and sat beside Mandy. He gave her a shaky smile. 'Whatever you do, don't mention the forbidden word when we get back!'

'What word?' Mandy asked.

'B-A-T-H.' James spelled it out.

Mandy grinned. Blackie might adore rolling in smelly mud, but he'd run a mile if he heard the word bath!

Back at Animal Ark, Mandy was soon warming herself in front of the fire in the sitting room, her hands cupped round a hot drink. She was in deep trouble.

'Will you never learn not to go charging into dangerous situations?' Emily Hope's voice rang with exasperation and concern.

'I'm with your mum on this one,' Adam Hope agreed. 'Whatever possessed you, Mandy? And after what happened the other day!'

'You would have done the same! I know you would!' Mandy protested. 'I had to save the deer from getting shot. If I hadn't chased them away, lots more of them would be dead by now.'

'Maybe Honey-Mum and Sprite with them,' James put in, trying to help.

'That's probably true,' admitted Mr Hope. 'But even so . . .'

'I have to agree with Mandy on this.' Unexpectedly, Sam Western spoke up. 'I'm grateful she acted as she did. By saving those deer, she also saved me a lot of money.'

James glanced at Mandy. 'Can you believe it? He's on our side for once!' he murmured. 'But only because there's money involved.'

Mandy raised her eyebrows.

Sam Western checked his wristwatch. 'I'll have to be getting back now. I need to go over to Walton to make a statement to the police.'

'Thanks for bringing Mandy and James back,' said Emily Hope. She went out to see Sam Western to the door.

Mandy looked at her dad. 'Sorry,' she said. 'I didn't mean to worry you and Mum.'

'You never do,' Adam Hope said with a sigh. 'What about the promise you made to keep out of those woods?'

'I know,' Mandy replied miserably. What could she say? She had been let off lightly last time because her ears had been hurt. This time her parents seemed really annoyed, and she didn't blame them.

Emily Hope had returned. She shook her head slowly, but she looked less angry. 'You'll turn us grey with worry. What are we going to do with you?' she said.

'Ground me for a week?' Mandy suggested.

'Sounds good to me,' her dad said. 'Emily?'

'And double chores?' said Emily Hope, a smile pulling at the corners of her mouth.

'Oh.' Mandy's face fell.

'I think being grounded for a week will do,' Adam Hope decided, winking at his wife.

'Thanks, Mum, Dad,' Mandy said, giving them

both a hug. 'Now that the deer are safe, I promise not to get into any more trouble!'

Adam Hope stroked his beard. 'Until the next time.'

'Hot soup and toast everyone?' asked Emily Hope.

'Yes, please!' Mandy and James said together.

'And then James and I have one muddy dog to bath!' Mandy said. 'Oh, no. I went and said it!'

She clapped both hands over her mouth. Too late. Blackie's ears had pricked up. He whined and crouched down so that his stomach brushed the floor. Then he crept towards the kitchen table.

Mandy looked at Blackie, who was trying to hide his stocky body behind the table leg. A laugh spilled out of her. 'Oh, Blackie, you're priceless! What are we going to do with you?'

'Bribery always works!' said James.

After tucking into their soup and toast, Mandy and James used dog biscuits to persuade Blackie into the veterinary residential unit. Blackie stood in the big sink at the back, which was used for washing animals.

Mandy began hosing Blackie with warm water. James squirted dog shampoo into his hand, then worked it into Blackie's thick coat. 'Being grounded isn't so bad. Blackie and I can always come over to see you,' he said.

Mandy nodded. 'And it's a small price to pay for knowing that Honey-Mum and Sprite are safe!'

Blackie seemed resigned to his ordeal. He sat quietly while he was soaped and rinsed. Then Mandy and James rubbed him briskly with a towel.

'This is the tricky bit,' puffed James, as he and Mandy struggled to lift Blackie out. Blackie kept still as they put him on to the floor. 'Good boy,' James praised him.

'Watch he doesn't shake himself now,' Mandy warned as she reached for the hair dryer. She switched it on and ruffled warm air through Blackie's wet coat.

James picked up a brush and Blackie was soon gleaming like polished coal.

'Ah! His fur's all fluffy, just like when he was a pup!' said James.

They both laughed. Blackie's ears were flat against his head. He gave them a disgusted look, but he wagged his tail.

Mandy gave him a cuddle. 'You look very smart!'

'Smart and brave!' James added proudly, ruffling Blackie's ears.

Seeing James with Blackie reminded Mandy of Echo and Julia. She'd hardly had time to think about them lately, with all the excitement of the poachers. But now things had calmed down she began worrying again about the deaf Dalmatian.

'I wonder if I should phone Julia?' she said. 'I bet she's feeling terrible.'

James nodded. 'Poor thing. It's a shame Echo's having to be re-homed, isn't it? I couldn't imagine not having Blackie.'

'No. Me neither,' Mandy agreed.

'Do you think there's any way the Hamptons will change their minds about keeping Echo?' asked James.

Mandy shook her head. 'They seemed pretty convinced that they couldn't cope with the extra training.'

James looked thoughtful. 'What we need is some way of showing Julia and her parents that re-training Echo isn't beyond them.'

A light seemed to come on in Mandy's head. 'Did anyone ever tell you you're brilliant, James Hunter?'

'All the time,' James joked.

'No, listen,' Mandy said eagerly. 'We could invite Julia and her parents to come to Animal

Ark. Then we can ask Elise to bring Maisy along as well.'

James looked impressed. 'So that they just happen to be here when the Hamptons arrive with Echo, you mean?'

'Yes,' Mandy said. 'If Julia's parents see how well Elise gets along with Maisy, they might change their minds about re-homing Echo.'

'Great idea. I'm glad I thought of it,' said James with a cheeky grin. 'It just might work.'

'Right.' Mandy couldn't wait to put their plan into action. 'As soon as we finish tidying up, I'll go and make the phone calls.'

Eleven

Elise arrived with Maisy on Thursday afternoon. Mandy had explained the situation to her over the phone. She went to the garden gate to greet them. 'Hi, Elise. Thanks for coming.'

'Hi, Mandy. Hi, Mr and Mrs Hope,' said Elise, her face lighting up in a smile. 'It's no problem. We're only too glad to help. I can imagine what Julia must be going through.'

'Yes. It's a difficult situation,' said Emily Hope. 'Let's hope Mandy's idea works.'

As soon as Maisy caught sight of Mandy, her tail wagged back and forth in greeting. Mandy patted her. 'Hello, beautiful.'

The Dalmatian looked gorgeous with her bright eyes and prancing steps. The liver-brown spots seemed to stand out on her glossy coat. Mandy had never seen her looking happier.

'The Hamptons should be here soon,' Mandy told Elise. 'James is coming too. But he had to cycle over to Walton to collect something first.'

In fact, James had been very mysterious about where he was going. Mandy wondered what he was up to.

Elise touched Maisy's head to get her attention. Then she pointed to the ground. Maisy sat down at once, still looking up at her owner's face. Elise unclipped her dog's lead and after a waiting for a moment, held up her hand and opened and closed her fingers in a snapping movement. Maisy leaped forward at once and began racing around the garden.

That must be the sign for 'off you go', Mandy thought. She watched, fascinated, as Elise threw her dog a ball. Maisy stretched up to catch it, then came running back to her owner with the ball in her mouth. Her tail wagged nineteen to the dozen.

Mandy joined in the game. She tossed the ball in the air and Maisy caught it easily. Mandy threw it again and it fell short. But Maisy didn't care. She dashed at the ball, pushed it along the grass with her nose, then batted it with her big paws. Mandy, Elise and Mr and Mrs Hope laughed.

'Maisy looks so happy, doesn't she?' Mandy said to her mum and dad.

'She certainly does,' said Mrs Hope. 'How's she getting on with her silent whistle?'

'Just great,' said Elise. 'I'm so grateful to you for telling me about it. Let me show you.'

As she was taking the whistle out of her pocket, Julia and her parents came into the garden. Julia's father held Echo on a very short lead. The Dalmatian had her head down and her tail was tucked between her legs.

Mandy was struck by the difference in the two dogs – Maisy, so happy and boisterous, and poor Echo looking timid and unhappy.

'Hi,' Julia greeted Mandy. She looked really miserable. 'Dad has to hold Echo now. I can't control her on the lead at the moment.'

'Julia, Mr and Mrs Hampton, this is Elise,' Mandy said.

'Hello, Elise. Nice to meet you,' Mr and Mrs Hampton replied.

Julia said hello too. Then she seemed to spot

Maisy. 'Is that your dog?' she said to Elise in surprise.

They all looked down the garden to where Maisy was playing happily with her ball.

'Yes,' Elise said. 'That's Maisy. And this must be Echo. She looks like a lovely dog.'

'She is,' said Julia, sounding pleased.

'Is it safe for your dog to be running around like that?' Mr Hampton asked. 'I mean, won't she run off if she gets the chance?'

Elise shook her head. 'Oh, no. Maisy's responded really well to her training. I'll call her over so that you can say hello.'

Julia frowned, but she looked intrigued. 'How are you going to do that? She can't hear you, can she?'

'Not if I shout to her, no,' agreed Elise. 'But most deaf animals still have some degree of hearing. Emily told me about a special silent whistle that only dogs can hear.' She showed Maisy's whistle to Julia. 'You can buy them in most pet shops.' Elise blew the whistle, while Julia and her parents watched closely.

Maisy's head shot up and she looked round. With her ears pricked, she trotted straight over to Elise.

'Good girl.' Elise took her dog's face in her hands to praise her.

'That's amazing,' said Julia's dad.

'I'd never have believed it,' Mrs Hampton agreed.

Julia didn't say anything for a moment. She was staring down at Echo. 'Could you blow it again, please?' she said excitedly to Elise.

'Of course.' Elise gave two short blasts.

Echo's ears swivelled. She looked up at Julia, her eyes bright and her mouth open as though she was smiling. She'd heard the whistle!

'Mum! Dad! She heard it!' Tears glittered in Julia's eyes.

'That's brilliant!' Mandy said, glancing up at her mum with a lump in her throat.

Mrs Hope patted her arm. 'It looks like it's going well,' she whispered.

Just then James arrived looking rather red in the face. He dumped his bike on the grass and came over. 'Hi! What's happening?'

Mandy started to explain, then Julia took over. 'Echo heard the dog whistle! Isn't it wonderful?' she said excitedly.

'Wow!' said James. 'That's great. And it looks as if Echo and Maisy have made friends too.' The two

Dalmatians were wagging their tails and sniffing each other. They made a handsome pair, Maisy with her liver and white colouring and Echo with her more traditional black and white spots.

'Why don't we let them play together?' suggested Elise. 'Echo will be quite safe. The garden is enclosed.'

Mr Hampton looked doubtful.

'Go on. Let her off the lead, Dad,' urged Julia. 'Poor Echo hasn't had a good run for days.'

Mr Hampton's face softened. He bent down to unclip the lead. 'I suppose it couldn't hurt.'

Maisy gave a joyful bark and darted away. Echo took off after her like a rocket. They dashed around play-biting and chasing each other.

'Echo looks just like her old self,' Julia said with delight. 'Look at her go!'

After watching the dogs play for a minute or two, James fished in his rucksack. He held out a coloured envelope to Mandy. 'Here you are. You tell me if these aren't prizewinners!'

'What?' Mandy opened the envelope and took out a pile of photographs. 'Oh, of course. I'd almost forgotten about these,' she said, beginning to leaf through them. Then her eyes opened wide as she looked at the photos of herself with Honey-Mum and Sprite. 'These are really lovely,' she said.

The doe and fawn stood in the dappled sunlight beneath the trees. Their coats looked glossy and healthy. In one of the photos, Sprite's graceful neck was reaching forward so that she could nuzzle Mandy's hand.

Mr and Mrs Hope admired the photographs. 'I think you stand a good chance of winning a prize with those,' Adam Hope commented.

'This one is definitely my favourite!' Mandy declared, holding up the one of herself stroking Sprite.

James grinned. 'I wanted to surprise you, so I got them developed by the one-hour service in Walton.'

Mandy laughed. 'So that was the great mystery! These are brilliant photos. But you know what? I reckon you have some pretty good subjects here. You should take some of Maisy and Echo playing together!'

'Yeah!' James agreed. 'Maybe we can arrange it sometime.'

Mandy gave him a hopeful look. 'Fingers crossed,' she whispered.

They looked down the garden at the Dalmatians. Maisy was crouching down on her front paws. Echo stood over her, tail wagging. She barked and pretended to nip Maisy's tail. Then the two of them took off again.

'Echo seems a lot less nervous, doesn't she?' said Julia.

'Yes,' Mandy answered. 'Maybe she's starting to get her confidence back.'

'Do you think so?' asked Julia.

'Mandy's right,' Mrs Hope said. 'And it will help Echo if you start to feel more relaxed too, then she won't feel so jumpy.'

Julia blinked at her. 'Do you mean that because we've all been so tense and worried, some of that has rubbed off on to Echo?'

'Yes,' Mrs Hope confirmed gently. 'That's the way it works with pets. But it works the other way too.'

So far, so good, Mandy thought. She had an idea, and turned to Elise. 'Can you blow the whistle to call Maisy to you again, please?'

'Sure,' said Elise. She blew the whistle.

Maisy's ears pricked and she looked around. She gave a short bark and ran towards Elise.

Mandy watched Echo closely. The Dalmatian

stood there, her ears twitching. She looked at
Elise who was making a big fuss of Maisy. Then
she looked at Julia. She whined softly, but stood
her ground.

'That's it, girl!' said Julia. She turned to Mandy.
'Echo can definitely hear the whistle. But she
doesn't realise she's supposed to come over.'

'Can we try that again, Elise?' Mandy asked.

Elise signed to Maisy to run down the garden
again. Maisy and Echo began playing together.
Elise let them become absorbed in their game for
a few moments, then this time, she asked Julia to
come and stand next to her. 'Ready?'

Julia bit her lip. 'OK.'

Elise blew the whistle. Once again Maisy ran
straight back up the garden to her owner. Echo's
ears pricked. She gave a short bark and dashed
after Maisy. Then she came right up to Julia, her
tail wagging eagerly.

'Give her lots of love and praise now, Julia!'
said Elise.

Julia didn't need telling twice. She crouched
down and cupped Echo's face as she had seen
Elise and Mandy do. 'Clever, girl. Oh, you clever
girl!' Julia's voice was choked with emotion as she
rubbed her cheek against Echo's face. 'Mum!

Dad! Did you see that? Wasn't she brilliant?'

Mrs Hampton looked delighted. She went over to Echo. Then she too crouched down and put her hands gently around Echo's face. 'Good girl!' she said. Echo wagged her tail and gave a proud little bark.

Mr Hampton went over to praise Echo with the same actions. 'She seems so alert now. I would never have believed it,' he declared. 'This is amazing!'

Elise beamed at Julia. 'Echo picked that up really quickly. She's obviously very intelligent. Do you want to try a couple of hand signals, Julia?'

Julia nodded eagerly.

'OK. If she runs to you, you do this to stop her jumping up.' Elise bent slightly and held her arms out in front with her palms raised as if to say 'stop'.

Julia copied her. 'That's easy,' she said.

'This is the signal for "sit".' Elise held her fingers together and pointed to the ground. 'Use a sort of jabbing movement.'

Julia practised. 'Like this?' She pointed her fingers at the floor.

Elise nodded. 'That's it. Well done.'

Julia looked pleased. 'I think I'm getting the hang of it. It's not as difficult as I thought.'

'It's natural to be nervous. I was at first,' Elise admitted. 'But look at us now! With patience and lots of practice, Echo will soon be as confident as Maisy.'

'Could we come for walks with you and Maisy sometimes?' Julia asked hesitantly.

Elise gave her a warm smile. 'Of course you can. We'd love that.'

'And they could use our garden for Echo's training, so Julia needn't worry about Echo getting out, couldn't they?' Mandy said to her mum.

Mrs Hope smiled. 'Any time!'

Julia beamed. She already seemed more confident – just like Echo.

'And James and me will help with Echo's training too, won't we?' Mandy spoke up again. James nodded.

Julia turned eagerly to her parents. 'Do you hear that? Everybody wants to help! Oh, we can keep Echo now, can't we?'

Mr and Mrs Hampton were smiling broadly. They glanced at each other, then looked at Adam and Emily Hope. 'With Elise giving us a bit of training advice, I think we could manage,' Julia's dad said at last.

'Yeah!' Julia jumped up and down. 'That's fantastic!'

Julia's mum stroked Echo. 'I think Echo deserves another chance. I hope she'll give us one too.'

'I thought you might be able to use this,' said Elise. She gave Julia a dog whistle. 'It's a spare one. You can use it until you get one for Echo.'

'Oh, thanks!' Julia looked delighted. She bent down and showed it to Echo. 'Look, this is for you!' Echo nudged the whistle with her black nose. Then she looked up at Julia and barked eagerly.

'I think she wants to try it out now!' laughed Julia.

Mandy thought she might burst with happiness. She grinned at her mum and dad, thrilled that her plan had worked. Echo and Julia were going to have so many good times together, and Mandy was sure it wouldn't be long before they were out enjoying long walks together in the dales again.

Labrador
on the
Lawn

One

'There it is!' Mandy Hope gasped as the car rounded a bend in the road. 'The lake! Look, James!'

'Where?' asked James, leaning forward and fumbling with his glasses. His dog, Blackie, sat between James and Mandy on the back seat. The Labrador's broad, whiskery muzzle lifted to the breeze as Mandy opened the window.

'Budge over,' James instructed his dog, who obligingly swapped places. He peered excitedly out of the window on Mandy's side. A vast stretch of slate-grey water stretched for as far as they could see along a wide, tree-lined valley.

'Wow,' said James. 'It's huge!'

Mandy's dad pulled the Land-rover to the side of the road and switched off the engine.

'Oh, it's gorgeous,' sighed Emily Hope, winding down the passenger window and taking a deep breath of cool air. 'Look, Adam,' she added, as her husband got out of the car, 'you can see the Langdales from here.' She pointed to a ridge of dramatic grey crags at the northern tip of the lake.

'And a yacht or two!' Adam Hope said longingly, gazing at the white sails that dotted the lake and giving the impressive mountains only a quick glance.

Mandy and James scrambled out of the car. Blackie bounded after them and James just managed to grab his collar before he took off down the steep bank.

'Poor Blackie!' Mandy smiled, smoothing the dog's sleek black head. 'We know you've been dying to get out and explore for an hour.'

'And so have you two!' laughed Mr Hope, adding, 'There's not much further to go now.'

They stood in silence for a moment, drinking in the scene. Beams of sunlight bounced off the silvery surface of Windermere. Mandy knew that the lake, at ten-and-a-half miles long, was the longest in England, but she hadn't been able to imagine its beauty. She thought it seemed peaceful and dramatic at the same time. She turned to her father, her eyes shining. 'I can't wait to get there.'

'Well, we'd better get on, then,' said Mr Hope, turning back purposefully towards the Land-rover. 'We're only a few miles from our cottage, according to the map.'

Mandy settled back into the hot car, feeling excitement fizz inside her. Their journey had begun that morning in their home village of Welford in Yorkshire. The Hopes had rented a cottage in the tiny village of Graythwaite, about three miles west of Windermere. James had been invited to come along to share the week's holiday, with Blackie as well, of course.

The visit to Cumbria had been Mandy's mum's idea. She and Mandy's father were vets who ran their own surgery, called Animal Ark. They'd had a very busy first half of the year.

'We need to get away,' Mrs Hope had suggested one Sunday morning, after a particularly challenging session trying to remove a hook and fishing line from the throat of an angry badger.

'Not anywhere far or exotic . . . just a nice, peaceful break.'

This was Mandy's first visit to the Lake District, so she and James had looked it up on the Internet. With the mountains, forests and waterfalls, it looked the perfect place for rambling with a good friend and his adventurous and lovable dog. Mandy slipped an arm round Blackie's shoulders and gave him a hug. His tongue lolled, making him look as though he was smiling. The tip of his tail twitched happily, because there wasn't room on the back seat to stand up and wag it properly.

Blackie's ears shot up as the road they were on led them into the deep shade of Grizedale Forest, as if he was listening to something. Mandy began to wonder if there were any animals peering back at them.

'Is the forest home to any particular animals, Mr Hope?' James raised his voice to be heard above the noise of the engine.

'Quite a few mammals, James,' replied Mandy's dad. 'I expect we'll be lucky enough to see roe deer, red squirrels, maybe a badger . . . and rabbits, of course.'

'Wonderful birds, too,' added Mrs Hope.

'Woodpeckers and jays, nuthatches and goldcrests and warblers.'

'And sheep,' said Adam Hope. 'Lots and lots of sheep. This is sheep farming country.'

James looked across Mandy and raised his eyebrows. They were both mad about animals.

'This is going to be fun,' Mandy smiled.

'You bet,' James responded. Blackie licked James's cheek and he wiped his face with the back of his hand. 'Get off, Blackie!' he protested. The dog sighed and tried to lie down but there wasn't room. As he shuffled around, he trod heavily on Mandy's hand.

'Ouch,' she said. 'Mum, I think Blackie needs to get out.'

'I'm sure you're right,' said Mrs Hope, turning to look at the panting Labrador.

Adam Hope nodded. 'Yes,' he said. 'But we can't let him loose just here. This is a fairly busy road. Let's go on for a bit and see if we can find a safe place for him to stretch his legs.'

Blackie was in luck. Just a mile further on, the trees ended, and Mr Hope was able to turn on to a narrow dirt road leading between some fields. He followed the twin tracks to a thicket of tall pines. Blackie began to whimper with delight.

'All right, all right,' said James, as Blackie began to scratch at the door. 'Can I let him out, Mr Hope?'

'It should be OK,' said Mandy's dad.

'It looks like pasture,' Emily Hope remarked, looking round, 'but I can't see a single sheep. That's good.'

'Let him go, James!' Mandy pleaded. Blackie's black nose twitched at the enticing smells coming from the lush grass around the car. He had managed to stand up on the seat, and was wagging his tail so hard it swiped at Mandy's face. James flung open the door and, with one bound, Blackie was out and following his eager nose into the undergrowth.

Emily Hope got out and stretched, while, from the back of the car, Mr Hope found the remains of the picnic lunch they'd had earlier. 'A chocolate biscuit, rather melted,' he announced, 'and two cans of drink. Anyone?'

'No thanks, Dad,' Mandy grinned, watching Blackie rolling happily in the dry grass.

'Keep an eye on him, won't you, James?' Mrs Hope warned, looking at Blackie. 'Farmers round here are bound to be very protective of their flocks. Dogs that worry sheep can be shot.'

'Yikes,' said James, pushing his glasses higher up on his nose. 'What a horrible thought.' He called to his dog, a look of concern on his face.

But Blackie wasn't listening. He was standing stock still, his ears pricked and one paw raised. His nose was raised to the breeze.

'Blackie!' said James, more sternly. 'Come here.'

Mr Hope put up a hand to shade his eyes from the sun. 'He's spotted something,' he said.

'Look, James!' cried Mandy, climbing on to the bumper of the car to get a better view. 'Rabbits!'

And with that, Blackie was off, streaking away over the crest of the hill, barking joyfully.

James groaned and set off in pursuit. 'I'll get him back,' he called as he broke into a trot. Mandy ran with him. She had no fear for the rabbits. She was certain that Blackie would be too slow to catch them. The big softie only wanted to play. James picked up speed and she raced beside him, yelling the dog's name.

In the pasture that stretched away on the other side of the hill, Mandy saw the rabbits scatter. One by one, they hopped neatly into nearby burrows in the ground and disappeared. Blackie pounced on a burrow, his tail wagging. He barked loudly and pushed his nose into the hole.

'Blackie!' puffed James, one hand pressed to his side as he gasped for breath.

And then Mandy's heart skipped a beat. Just beyond the burrow was a flock of sheep. She caught hold of James's sleeve to alert him. 'Hang on,' she said. 'Don't yell at him any more.'

James turned to her and frowned. 'Why not?' he panted.

Mandy pointed. The sheep had raised their heads and were staring balefully at the big dog. They began to bleat and fuss, shifting warily and turning in confused circles. The panic spread through the flock like wildfire, and a few began to run.

Blackie backed out of the rabbit hole and looked at the sheep. He appeared to be sizing them up, and Mandy's heart began to thump harder.

'James . . . he wouldn't . . . would he?' she gasped.

James groaned again. 'I hope not,' he said. But he sounded worried. Then he groaned even louder. 'Oh no, now we're in trouble – look!'

As the flock began to scatter, James had seen a man crouching. He had been attending to a sheep, which lay on its side at his feet. He let the animal go and it went lumbering off. Then he stood up and looked about him.

James and Mandy froze. 'Has he got a gun?' James whispered.

'I don't know,' Mandy whispered back. She looked back up the hill for her parents, but she couldn't see the tree or the Land-rover from where she was.

Blackie's attention switched from the sheep to the stranger who had popped up among them. He wagged his tail in greeting and trotted towards the man to say hello.

Mandy tried waving at the farmer, a smile on her face.

'Clear off!' he shouted. 'I don't want that dog frightening my flock. Call him back, will you?'

'I'm very sorry,' Mandy shouted back. 'He wouldn't do any harm, honestly.'

'Can't take that chance, I'm afraid.' The farmer waved his arms at Blackie, who stopped. He seemed puzzled by the firm tone of the man's voice. His tail drooped and his ears went down.

'Blackie!' James used his sternest voice. 'Here – now!'

The Labrador turned and walked back to James.

He looked rather sorry for himself, and Mandy's heart melted.

'Don't scold him, James,' she said. 'Let's just go, as quickly as we can.'

'You were lucky this time,' remarked Adam Hope, as they rejoined the main road. 'We must make absolutely sure Blackie doesn't go wandering off again.'

James was flushed pink from his dash over the hill. He was still cross with Blackie, who had relaxed on the back seat, looking out of the window as though he hadn't a care in the world.

'I hope the cottage garden is fenced,' said Emily Hope. 'I didn't think to ask when I booked it through the agency.'

'Who owns the cottage?' Mandy asked.

'I've no idea,' replied her mother. 'The woman at the agency didn't say. I think the owners are just letting it out for the summer.'

'This is the road,' said Mr Hope, spotting a signpost. 'Sunny Brow Lane.'

Mrs Hope looked at the map. 'We want number four,' she reminded him.

Mandy sat up straight. She couldn't wait to see the cottage. It had such a lovely name – Laurel

Cottage. She hoped it would be really old, filled with interesting nooks and crannies.

She wasn't going to be disappointed, she realised, as her dad pulled up outside a tiny whitewashed cottage that stood on its own in a rambling, flower-filled garden. Grizedale Forest stretched out on all sides, with a silver glimmer just through the trees below showing where the lake was.

Ivy covered the walls of the cottage, reaching almost to the chimney. The split front door, painted butter yellow, and tiny, wooden-framed windows gave it the appearance of a doll's house.

'Oh!' Mandy gasped. 'It's lovely!'

'Will we all fit in it, do you think?' James frowned. 'It looks rather small.'

'It has three bedrooms,' said Adam Hope, looking doubtful.

'We'll be fine,' Mrs Hope told them. 'Come on, let's unpack and put the kettle on.'

Mandy jumped out and ran up to the front door. It had a rusted old brass knocker shaped like a lion's claw. James let it fall with a resounding thud.

'I've got the key,' Mrs Hope said. 'And it really will be a squash if there's anyone else staying here! Let's leave Blackie in the car for a bit, just until we investigate the garden.'

James nodded. 'Good idea.' From the back seat of the Land-rover, Blackie howled his disapproval at being left behind.

Mandy unlocked the front door and went in. She found herself in a little hall, leading to a living room, with a flagstone floor and shaggy rugs, a big friendly-looking fireplace and a mantelpiece piled with interesting ornaments. A framed painting of an otter hung over the fireplace. Mandy went closer to admire it. The animal was poised on a rock in a river, looking intently into its depths. Mandy smiled. She loved otters. But there was more to see in the cottage, and she raced after James, up a steep wooden staircase to the bedrooms above.

'One,' Mandy counted, pushing open a wooden door. 'This has got a double bed so it can be mum and dad's room. Two, small but nice . . . and right opposite, bedroom number three! Which one would you like, James?'

'This one, please,' said James, admiring a small painting of a fleet of yachts on the wall above the bed.

'Good,' said Mandy happily, 'because I like the one overlooking the front garden.'

'That's settled then,' James said. 'I'd better go

and see if it's OK to let Blackie out. He'll be hot in the car.'

'I'll come with you,' Mandy offered.

Mrs Hope was in the kitchen, filling the kettle, and Mandy's dad was just coming through the front door with some of the luggage from the boot of the car.

'I'll help in a minute, Mr Hope,' James said cheerfully. 'I'll just see that it's safe to let Blackie out.'

'Fine, James,' Mr Hope grinned. 'Great little place, isn't it?'

'It's brilliant,' Mandy smiled. 'It's a storybook cottage.'

'Are you coming, Mandy?' called James.

'Yes!' said Mandy, squeezing past her father and out of the door.

James had begun to pick his way between two overgrown flowerbeds. He and Mandy walked slowly round the edge of the garden, checking there was enough of a fence to stop Blackie leaping off into the meadow.

'There's a jungle of thorny bushes here,' Mandy said. 'I don't think Blackie would try to get through this!'

'I don't know,' James frowned. 'He's bright

enough to work out how to escape if he wants to.'

'And bright enough to have squeezed out of a car window!' said Mandy, laughing.

'What!' said James. 'Where is he?'

'Over there,' Mandy said, standing on tiptoe and pointing over the flowerbed.

James shaded his eyes with one hand. Only the glossy black tip of Blackie's tail could be seen, waving like a banner as it disappeared round the side of the cottage.

'Honestly!' said James, exasperated. 'Will that dog *ever* learn to do as he's told?' They pushed their way out of the overgrown part of the garden and ran down the stone path that led along the side of the cottage. But Mandy stopped dead when she got to the corner.

There were *two* dogs on the lawn! Standing nose-to-nose with Blackie was a sleek, golden-haired Labrador.

Two

'Now where did you come from?' Mandy whispered.

'It's another Labrador!' exclaimed James.

'I can see that! Isn't she beautiful?' Mandy declared.

'Not as nice as Blackie,' James responded loyally. 'But she's pretty, I'll give you that.'

The dog was slightly smaller than Blackie, with a narrow tapering face the colour of butter. She had darker markings around her caramel-coloured eyes, and her ears were pale gold.

Blackie stood stock still for a moment, staring at the strange dog. Then he wagged his tail hesitantly.

The golden Labrador lay down submissively. Blackie seemed a bit puzzled at first, but, as Mandy and James watched, the bigger dog's playful nature got the better of him. His whole body began to sway with the force of his wagging tail. He gave a little prance, then stretched down to sniff the dog's face.

'Uh-oh,' James said quietly. 'Do you suppose she'll mind Blackie being a pest? I mean, do you think they'll fight?'

'Fight!' Mandy echoed. 'That's not likely. Labradors are the best-natured dogs in the world, for a start, and secondly . . . it's a girl!' Mandy glanced at James and grinned.

The mystery dog was still lying on the lawn, her pale gold tail wagging gently. She waited patiently while Blackie circled her, sniffing at her coat. His inspection complete, Blackie seemed completely overcome with joy at finding a new friend. He rolled over on to his side, paddling all four paws at her like a puppy.

'You silly dog,' muttered James.

'They like each other!' Mandy declared happily. 'Come on, James. Let's go and say hello.'

The Labrador looked up as Mandy and James

approached. She cocked her head and her tail stopped wagging.

'Hang on, Mandy,' said James. 'She seems a bit wary. Shouldn't we wait till her owner turns up?'

'What if she doesn't have an owner?' Mandy pointed out. 'After all, there aren't any neighbours round here, and there were no cars parked in the lane. She might be lost.'

When they were just a couple of metres away, the Labrador stood up. She looked directly at Mandy, her brown eyes soft. She limped a single step, then stopped and raised one front paw.

'James! She's injured,' Mandy cried. She crouched on to her haunches, making herself small and unthreatening, the way her parents had taught her, and gently stretched out one hand. 'Hello, you lovely girl,' she said.

James was distracted by Blackie, who had bounded over to him and was standing on his back legs trying to lick James's face.

'Down!' James commanded, smoothing Blackie's head. He looked over to see how Mandy was getting on. Mandy was stroking the dog's head, still talking softly.

'You've hurt yourself,' she told her. 'You need

help with that paw, and you've come to the right place.'

'Do you think that she'll follow us into the cottage?' asked James.

'I'm not sure,' Mandy replied. 'She seems friendly enough but she's also a bit nervous.'

'We don't want her to run off,' mused James, who walked across the grass and knelt down beside Mandy to get a better look. The Labrador was in good condition, her coat sleek and shiny and her ribs well covered. 'She's not been going hungry,' he observed, pointing to her plump pink tummy.

'I don't know where she could suddenly have appeared from.' Mandy felt puzzled. She tried taking a closer look at the paw the dog was holding up, but the Labrador pulled away at once and warned Mandy off with a soft growl.

'She's really in pain!' Mandy exclaimed. 'James, will you go and fetch Mum or Dad? I'll stay here with her.'

'Right.' James sounded very purposeful. He backed away slowly so as not to startle the dog, then, when he was well clear, he sprinted for the back door to the cottage. Blackie stayed with Mandy and his new friend.

The yellow Labrador gazed after James as he disappeared indoors. Mandy tried to look at the underside of her paw, without going too close, but she couldn't see anything. She held the wriggling Blackie at arm's length, and was relieved when her father came striding out of the cottage, James hurrying behind him.

'What have we got here? I can't believe you've managed to find another animal in need of help just minutes after our arrival!'

Mandy nodded as her dad approached, walking

slowly so as not to alarm the dog. 'No collar,' he remarked, setting down his veterinary bag on the grass. He held out a gentle hand and the yellow Labrador looked up sorrowfully as Mr Hope bent over her.

'Poor girl,' he said soothingly. 'Will you let me see that paw?'

'I tried to have a look,' Mandy told her dad. 'But she wouldn't let me touch it.'

Adam Hope reached gently for the dog's foot. The Labrador snatched it away, but not before he'd seen enough to know what was needed. 'Wow, that's quite a cut she's got there. It must be very uncomfortable for her.'

'What are you going to do, Mr Hope?' James was standing a little way off, hanging on to Blackie.

'I'll have to give her a sedative, I think, to calm her. Then she'll let us bring her inside and treat her wound,' he said.

While Mr Hope prepared an injection, Mandy's mum arrived with a handful of Blackie's treats. 'What a gorgeous dog!' she exclaimed. 'I wonder where she came from?'

Blackie jumped out of James's grip and pushed his eager nose into Mrs Hope's palm. 'No, Blackie,' she laughed. 'These aren't for you.' James ran up and grabbed Blackie's collar again. The dog seemed determined to get as close to their visitor as he could!

Emily Hope gave the biscuits to Mandy, who offered one to the yellow Labrador. She stretched her neck out and accepted it gratefully. Her nose worked as she lay on the grass, looking for more.

'Oh, Mum, she's hungry, poor girl,' Mandy said.

'I expect she's been wandering around for a while,' said Mrs Hope. 'That doesn't look like a fresh wound. But her coat is in good condition so I shouldn't think she's a long-term stray.'

The Labrador was still busy sniffing for more biscuits, when Adam Hope gently slid his needle into the muscle at the back of her neck. As the syringe released the sedative drug, she looked round, surprised, then shook her head vigorously.

'Good,' said Mr Hope, straightening up. 'It won't be long before she's dozy enough to bring indoors. Then we'll see what we can do with that paw.'

It took just a few minutes before the golden Labrador began to get sleepy. Mandy stroked the top of her head. She could see the confusion in the dog's brown eyes and felt a pang of sympathy. She hoped the dog knew they only wanted to help.

'She's going all wobbly,' James whispered, as the Labrador struggled to stand up and took a faltering step. She flopped down on her side and stretched out with a long, contented sigh.

'Now,' said Emily Hope. 'Let's take her inside.'

Mr Hope bent down and scooped the Labrador into his arms. He held her round her chest and tail, and her chin rested on his arm.

Emily Hope had gone into the cottage ahead of them and spread several sheets of newspaper on the big wooden table in the kitchen. Mandy opened the kitchen door wide enough for Mr Hope to squeeze through with the dog lying in his arms. He laid her gently on the tabletop. In a moment, Blackie had his front paws on the table, craning his neck to sniff at her.

'I think we'd best keep Blackie out of the way, James – just for now,' said Emily Hope.

'Right,' said James, looping his fingers through Blackie's collar. 'I'll put him back in the car, shall I?'

Adam Hope nodded as he scrubbed his hands under a running tap at the kitchen sink.

'And make sure he can't get out of a window!' Mandy added with a smile, before turning her full attention to the Labrador on the table. Using a pair of small sterile scissors, Mrs Hope had started clipping the fur from between the pads on the dog's front paw. Tufts of soft yellow hair fell on to the newspaper, exposing a deep cut on the tender place just above the pad.

'That looks sore,' remarked Adam Hope. 'My guess is that she's made the cut worse by walking around on it. It'll need stitching.'

James slipped back into the kitchen. He stood beside Mandy and stroked the dog's head. She was awake, and blinked up at them, but she didn't seem to mind about the strangers attending to her paw.

'Sweet girl,' Mandy murmured, feeling how velvety her ears were. She helped her mother by taking the scissors from her when the fur had been clipped away, and watched as the cut was thoroughly cleaned with sterile liquid on gauze. Then Adam Hope stepped up with his needle threaded, ready to stitch the wound. First, Mandy knew, the dog would be given a shot of local anaesthetic, so she wouldn't feel any pain.

When Mandy's mum slipped a fine needle into

the paw, the Labrador appeared not to notice, but lay still, looking quite comfortable. Mandy kept a gentle hand on her head. She watched the strange loops of the needle and passed her father the scissors as each stitch was neatly finished and cut.

'There,' he said, when the last one was complete. 'A few antibiotics to make sure you don't have any infection, young lady, and you'll be as right as rain.'

Mr Hope heaved the Labrador into his arms again, and Mandy led the way into the sitting room to find a comfortable place where the dog could lie. 'Why don't we put her here?' she suggested, patting the rug that lay in front of the hearth.

The dog's head lolled as Mr Hope carefully laid her down and she sighed again, closing her eyes.

'I expect she'll want to sleep for a while, Mandy,' Mrs Hope called. She had rolled up the newspaper and was spraying disinfectant on to the kitchen table.

'OK,' Mandy replied. 'I'll just keep an eye on her, though.'

James sat on the floor beside Mandy. 'Where do you think she's come from?' he asked. 'And what are we going to do with her?'

'I can't think,' said Mandy. 'She's a beautiful dog. She must be somebody's pet. I'm sure someone out there is searching for her even now.'

'We should give her a name, just for the time she's here with us,' James suggested.

'Yes,' Mandy smiled. 'She's too lovely not to have a name. What do you think it should be?'

'How about Serena?' said James.

Mandy wrinkled her nose. 'Sounds like a name for a princess,' she teased. 'What about Goldie? She has such a wonderful golden coat, after all.'

'Goldie!' James said approvingly. 'Yes, that's it. Goldie.' He tried the name again. It seemed to suit the sleeping Labrador perfectly.

Adam Hope came in and lowered himself into an easy chair. He looked down at his patient. 'She couldn't be in better hands, that's for sure.' He smiled at Mandy and James. 'But what are we going to do with her now?'

'I think she's lost,' Mandy said.

'But what if she's been abandoned?' James looked worried. 'You know, dumped by someone who doesn't want her any more?'

'Well, whatever happened to her, she hasn't been alone for very long,' Mr Hope reassured him. 'She's in good condition, and that suggests to me that she's wandered away from her owners rather than been dumped.'

'We've decided to call her Goldie,' Mandy told him.

'Some of the locals might know of her,' suggested Emily Hope, coming in from the kitchen with two cups of tea. 'Why don't you and James walk into the village and ask around?'

'That's a great idea, Mum!' Mandy agreed. 'Is it OK if we go now?'

'I should think so. It's not very far,' Mr Hope said, looking at his watch. 'You could try asking at the post office first.'

'Yes!' James jumped up and Goldie's eyes flickered sleepily. Just then, a volley of shrill barking could be heard from the direction of the car.

'Oops, that's Blackie,' said James. 'He'd like a walk. Shall we take him along?'

Mrs Hope picked up Blackie's lead from a side table. 'You'd better take this,' she grinned. 'And don't let him off for a minute!'

James chuckled while Mandy tied the laces on her trainers. 'Which way is it?' she asked.

'You can't go wrong.' Emily Hope was looking at the map they had used to find the cottage. 'The village is back the way we came, right along this road, then left at the telephone box.'

'I know where you mean,' Mandy nodded.

Mr Hope handed Mandy some money. 'Will you buy a loaf of bread, love?' he asked. 'I'm sure the post office will have a village shop as well, like the one in Welford does.'

'Sure,' said Mandy. 'We'll do our best to find out something about Goldie as well and be back before it gets dark.'

James was already at the door. 'Come on, Mandy,' he called.

Mandy could tell he was as eager as she was to solve the mystery of Goldie's appearance on their lawn. She snatched up her jumper from the back of the chair. 'Right,' she said. 'Let's go.'

Three

Blackie was so pleased to be let out of the car that he jumped up with his paws on James's chest and tried to lick his nose. Then, as though he suddenly remembered the pretty golden Labrador he had met in the garden, he turned and raced back towards the cottage. Mandy and James chased after him.

'Hey! Come back here!' James shouted.

Blackie had come to a stop by the closed front door. He stood and looked up at James, his tail wagging hard. 'Blackie,' Mandy explained patiently, 'you're coming with us for a walk. You can't go in there. She's not very well.' She clipped the lead on to the dog's collar and handed it to James. Blackie followed at his heels.

It was a warm afternoon and the sky above was a clear blue. Mandy and James went out of the gate to the cottage and turned left down the narrow tarred road towards the village. Mandy hadn't realised how high up they were, but now she could see the towering peaks her mum had spoken of, and a ring of gentle green hills that spread magically all around them.

'There's the lake!' said James, stopping abruptly to point and making Blackie cough as the lead jerked tight.

'This is a great place,' Mandy said happily. Then, more seriously, she added, 'I just hope we can find Goldie's owner before too long.'

'We will,' James said with determination. 'She's such a beautiful dog. I'm sure somebody in Graythwaite will know her.'

After ten minutes, with James having to stop frequently while Blackie dragged him off to investigate a special scent along the side of the road, they rounded a corner to see the village before them. A pretty church stood at the far end of a long, narrow street. There were houses along either side of the road, and from where they were standing, Mandy could see two shops with big front windows that curved into the street.

'We'll make a start there,' said Mandy, heading for the familiar red sign that announced a post office.

The door was locked. A sign in the window read: 'Closed. Opening hours: 9am–1pm.'

'It's closed,' said James, disappointed. He rattled the door.

'Don't,' Mandy warned. 'We might set off an alarm or something.' She cupped her hands round her face to block out the glare from the sun and looked in. There wasn't anybody about. 'That's a shame,' she said.

She stepped back and noticed a photograph of an otter on a poster taped inside the window. She was immediately drawn to the small fuzzy head and beady bright eyes. The little animal lay on its back in water, its front paws touching over its chest. 'Another otter!' she said.

'Where?' James sounded surprised, and looked up and down the street.

'Not there, silly!' Mandy laughed. 'In there – on the poster.' She tapped lightly on the glass.

'Oh!' James looked in. 'It's a pup,' he said, grinning. 'I love otters.'

'So do I. They're so sweet,' Mandy smiled. 'Lakeside Otter Sanctuary,' she read aloud from the poster. 'A special environment set up for the rehabilitation of rescued otters.'

'Newly opened in Lakeside,' James read on. 'I wonder where that is?'

Mandy turned to him, her eyes wide with excitement. 'James!' she exclaimed. 'Lakeside's not far from here. I remember driving through it on the way to Windermere. We could ask Mum and Dad to take us there!'

'That would be great,' James agreed. Together they gazed at the poster, trying to make out the small writing along the bottom of the paper.

'Excuse me?'

Mandy jumped. A woman had quietly come up behind them. She wore a wide-brimmed straw hat and in her hand she held several postcards.

'Hello,' Mandy said brightly.

'Is it open?' the woman asked. 'The post office, I mean.'

'No,' James chipped in. 'We missed it. It shut at one o'clock.'

'Oh, dear, I did want to get these off today,' the woman said. 'I'll be back in Buckinghamshire before they reach my brother at this rate.'

'You're a visitor to the Lake District?' Mandy asked, hoping the woman wouldn't think her rude for prying. She hurried on with her question. 'You see, my friend and I have found a dog . . .'

'It's a Labrador,' James put in. 'A yellow Labrador.'

'And we don't know where it came from,' Mandy continued. 'We were hoping someone in the post office might be able to help us.'

The woman adjusted her hat and looked down at Blackie. 'Yellow?' she echoed, sounding puzzled.

Mandy grinned. 'Oh no, not *this* dog. This is Blackie. He belongs to my friend James.'

Blackie had found a small piece of waxy paper and was lying with it between his front paws, ripping it to shreds with his teeth. When he heard his name he sprang up. His tail began to thump happily and he strained on his leash to sniff the woman's hand. James tugged his dog back as she backed quickly away.

'I'm sorry,' she said. 'I'm not very good with dogs. I come out in a frightful rash from their fur, you see.'

'Oh dear,' said Mandy, quickly helping James to keep Blackie away. 'We'll let you go then.'

'I'm sorry I can't help,' the woman said, turning to leave. 'Perhaps you could try the bed and breakfast I'm staying in? Caleb's Cottage. It's just across the street.'

'Thanks,' Mandy smiled. At her feet, Blackie had snuffled up the last scrap of paper and was holding it in his mouth.

'Bye,' James called to the woman, while trying to pull the dirty wrapper out of Blackie's mouth. He straightened up, and frowned at his slimy fingers. 'Yuck,' he said, wiping his hand on his jeans.

'Let's try the bed and breakfast next,' Mandy said. 'I'll go in. You can wait here with Blackie, if you like?'

'Right,' James agreed.

Mandy crossed the road. There was very little traffic, even though it was the holiday season. She spotted a sign above an arched doorway reading, *Caleb's Cottage.* She pushed open the front door and found herself in a narrow hallway. There was a small white desk with a telephone on it but no one was about. Mandy wondered what to do. Should she call out?

'Can I help you?' said a voice.

Mandy jumped and turned. A young man

wearing a green-and-white striped apron had appeared in a doorway. He dabbed his perspiring forehead with the sleeve of his shirt.

'I hope so,' Mandy began, feeling a little shy. 'I've come on holiday to Graythwaite with my parents. We're staying for a week in Laurel Cottage and we've found a dog. It just appeared . . .'

'A dog?' he repeated, coming towards Mandy and looking interested. Her spirits rose.

'Yes, a yellow Labrador,' she confirmed. 'It's lost, we think . . .'

'I'd like to help,' he said kindly. 'I love dogs. I'm the new chef here. I'm from London and I haven't had a chance to meet any of the locals yet – or their dogs.'

'Oh,' Mandy said, her heart sinking.

'There's an RSPCA office here, I know that,' the young man went on helpfully. 'You could take the dog there. They'd put it in kennels for you, until they can find it a new home.'

'Thanks, but I think we'll go on trying to find her owner,' Mandy said.

'Well, good luck then.' The chef smiled at her. 'I'm sorry I couldn't help.'

'That's all right,' Mandy smiled back. 'Thanks, anyway.'

As she was waiting to cross the street to where James was waiting, she saw her friend wave to a boy pedalling away on a bicycle.

'Any luck?' James asked, as Mandy joined him. Blackie wagged his tail and pushed a wet nose into the palm of her hand.

'No.' Mandy shook her head. 'I spoke to the

chef but he's new here too.'

'I stopped a boy.' James pointed to the departing back of the cyclist as he sped off round the corner. 'He's camping with his family. He did say he'd seen a golden Labrador who belonged to one of the families on the site.'

'Hmm,' said Mandy. 'There's no telling if it might have been Goldie, though.'

'Hang on a minute. How about this for an idea?' James looked triumphant. 'Why don't we take a photograph of Goldie and pin copies all around the place?'

'That's a brilliant idea!' Mandy agreed. 'And we could make posters too! Come on, let's go back and do it right away.'

'Um, aren't we forgetting something?' James shook the loose change in his pocket.

Mandy looked blank, then suddenly remembered. 'The bread!'

Blackie seemed delighted to be on the move. He trotted ahead, pulling at his lead and looking round with great interest.

'Here's the shop. I'll go in,' James offered, handing Blackie's lead to Mandy. She gave him the money.

'Brown, please,' she told him.

'OK, and I might ask the person behind the counter if they know of Goldie, too.'

'Good thinking,' Mandy nodded her approval.

Blackie sat down again and sighed heavily. Mandy rumpled his ear. 'Not much of a walk for you, is it, boy?'

James was only a minute, and he came out of the shop shaking his head.

'What?' asked Mandy.

'I tried to ask, but the shop suddenly got very busy. I just didn't get a chance. There was a lot of pushing and shoving behind me.' He sounded frustrated.

Mandy smiled at him. 'Bad luck,' she said. 'Never mind. Let's go home and plan our poster campaign. I'm starving anyway. Aren't you?'

'Yes,' James agreed, taking Blackie's lead.

'And I'm dying to see how our lovely Goldie's getting on,' said Mandy.

As soon as James and Mandy arrived back at Laurel Cottage, Mrs Hope put her head round the door of the kitchen. 'Hi,' she said. 'Did anybody know anything about our mystery Labrador?'

'No.' Mandy handed her mum the bread, then kicked off her shoes.

'Nothing but tourists in the village,' added James, looking forlorn.

'Well, that's what we are, too,' Emily Hope smiled.

'How is she?' Mandy glanced at the hearthrug, but Goldie wasn't there. She looked back at her mother, puzzled.

'She's out in the garden with Dad,' said Mrs Hope. 'Go and say hello, if you like. Make sure Blackie doesn't knock her off her feet, James. She's not very steady yet.'

Mandy and James went out of the kitchen door. Blackie shook his head vigorously to make sure he was free of his lead, then scrambled after them.

Adam Hope was sitting on the lawn reading a book. From time to time, he looked up to watch the Labrador snuffling around him, limping heavily, with her injured paw held off the ground.

'Dad!' Mandy called. 'We're back.'

Mr Hope looked up and smiled. 'Did you find Goldie's owner?' he asked.

'No. We couldn't even find a person who *lives* here,' Mandy told him.

'That's the trouble,' said Mr Hope. 'At this time

of year, locals are vastly outnumbered by tourists.'

'Uh-oh,' James said warningly. 'Look out . . .'

Blackie had spotted Goldie and was racing towards her. Then, just as Adam Hope got to his feet to try and prevent a collision, Blackie seemed to sense that pouncing on his friend wouldn't be a good idea. Instead, he lay down on his tummy and put his head on his paws, wagging his tail.

Goldie's ears pricked up. Hopping on her three good paws, she walked up to the black dog and stood over him. Blackie stood up to sniff at her chest, and turned in a circle, inviting her to join in a game.

'Hold your horses, young man.' Adam Hope stepped in and took hold of Blackie's collar. 'She's not well enough for a dance just yet.' James ran forward and hung on to his dog.

Mr Hope rummaged in the pocket of his shorts for a treat. 'It's best we go inside,' he said. 'She needs to rest that leg and I don't want her wandering off, either.'

Goldie limped after Adam Hope, her front paw held high. Blackie was happy to follow his new friend into the kitchen of the cottage. Mrs Hope had just put down a bowl of fresh water and both dogs lapped thirstily. When she was finished, Goldie went to the front door and wagged her tail expectantly, looking over her shoulder at them with pleading brown eyes.

'She wants to leave!' Mandy said sadly.

'Well, she can't,' Emily Hope shook her head firmly as she laid a steaming vegetable casserole on the kitchen table. 'She needs to rest, overnight at the very least. We'll make a plan in the morning. Come and have something to eat now.'

Mandy and James washed their hands and sat down at the table. Blackie had found his favourite toy, a rubber bone that had been well chewed. He padded over to the door and presented it to Goldie, sweetly laying it at her paws.

'Ah,' Mandy sighed. 'They're so lovely together.'

'Mandy and I have decided to make a poster that will help us find Goldie's owner,' announced James.

'That's a good idea,' said Emily Hope.

'We thought we might make a few of them,' Mandy added. 'We'll stick them up around the village.'

'We thought we could take a few photographs of her, too,' James said.

'Yes,' said Mandy. 'Somebody might recognise her.'

'Do you think that her owners are still around?' James asked. 'I mean, they could have been tourists too, and now they might have gone back to where they came from.'

'I can't believe that anyone would give up a dog like Goldie quite so easily,' said Mr Hope.

'She's a real mystery,' Mandy remarked.

'We'll find her owners,' said Emily Hope, spooning some casserole on to James's plate. 'I'm sure we will.'

Mandy turned to look at the two Labradors. Blackie was lying beside Goldie on the front doormat.

'I hope so,' she said. 'I *really* hope so.'

After supper, Mandy and James made a bed for Goldie in the kitchen. The Labrador seemed restless and unsure, and Blackie hovered over her, as though he was worried. Time and time again, Goldie hobbled to the front door, looking up expectantly at Mandy with big, sad eyes.

'No, girl,' Mandy said, smoothing her head.

'You must stay here, just until we can find out where you belong.'

Finally, with an air of defeat, Goldie settled down on the blanket Mandy had spread out. As Mandy sat with her, the dog's eyes started to close.

'Go to sleep,' Mandy whispered, letting her hand travel down the dog's silky coat, all the way to the base of her tail.

'Goodnight, Goldie.' James bent down to pat her. Blackie gave a final prance, still trying to coax his friend into a game of chase. But Goldie had fallen asleep, and James led him away.

Adam and Emily Hope were looking at guidebooks in the sitting room, making notes on a pad of paper.

'I'd like to set aside a day for a spot of sailing,' Mr Hope was saying when Mandy came in.

'Goldie's asleep,' she announced. 'James has taken Blackie upstairs to his room.'

'Good idea,' Mrs Hope smiled. 'We don't want any mad games in the night.'

Mandy yawned. 'Are there sheets for the beds, Mum?'

'It's all done, love,' her mother replied. 'Have a good night and I expect we'll all be up bright and early to see how Goldie is.'

Mandy nodded. 'She'll be fine,' she said. 'She's a good girl. But I really hope we find her owner soon. Somebody must be missing her badly!'

Four

Mandy woke to the sound of scratching. It took her several seconds to work out from which direction in the cottage the noise was coming, and what it could be.

And then she realised.

'Blackie!' she chuckled. She looked at her watch. It was six-thirty, early enough for her to do her best to try and keep him quiet, and allow her parents to sleep on. She slipped out of bed and across the hall to James's room. The wooden floorboards felt cold and slippery under her feet. Blackie stopped scratching as he sensed her approach and gave a particularly heart-rending whimper of frustration.

'James!' Mandy hissed, opening the door just a crack. Blackie's brown eyes looked up at her. James had closed the curtains across his window and the room was still quite dark. All Mandy could see was a tuft of brown hair sticking out from a tangle of sheets and blankets.

Blackie was thrilled to see her. Mandy put out her hands to him and he licked her fingers. 'Silly boy,' she said, tickling him under his chin. 'I'm sure you're longing to see Goldie, but you must be quiet! We'll let you out in a minute.' Mandy prodded a bump under the blanket. 'Wake up, James.'

The bump groaned. A hand appeared and groped on the bedside table for the pair of glasses. James put them on and sat up, blinking, looking around as if he couldn't remember where on earth he was.

'Blackie's going to wake the whole house,' Mandy told him, grinning. 'He wants to go downstairs and find Goldie.'

'What time is it?' James mumbled.

'Early – six-thirty,' said Mandy, pulling Blackie away from the door. He'd managed to leave a claw mark on the paintwork already. 'James, do something! Shall I let him out?'

'We'd better check on Goldie first,' James said sensibly. 'We don't want Blackie leaping on her and knocking her over if she's still feeling poorly.'

'No,' Mandy agreed. 'But if we leave him in here, he'll scratch the door to shreds.'

James got out of bed and reached for Blackie's lead. 'There,' he said, clipping it on to Blackie's collar. 'Come on, let's all go downstairs and see how the patient is.'

The staircase creaked loudly and Blackie coughed as he strained at the lead. Mandy was certain her mother and father would be wide awake by now, but it couldn't be helped. In the kitchen, Goldie was drinking from the water bowl. She was delicately poised on three legs, holding her front paw high off the floor. She jumped and staggered when James, Mandy and Blackie burst through the door.

Blackie was overjoyed to see the Labrador again, but James held him back on a short lead. 'Easy, boy,' he said, sympathetically.

'It's all right, Goldie,' Mandy crooned, stroking her. 'It's only us. How are you feeling?'

Goldie wagged her tail and lay down on her side. Mandy looked at her raised paw and

gasped. 'James! She undid all of the stitches.
Look!'

Goldie's cut had opened up again, and had
started to bleed.

James knelt beside her, one arm outstretched to
stop Blackie pouncing on her. 'Yikes,' he said.

'Will you call my dad?' asked Mandy. 'I'll stay
with her.'

Without a word, James scrambled to his feet and
pounded noisily up the stairs.

Mandy's head swivelled between Goldie and
Blackie as she anxiously tried to keep an eye on
both. Goldie had begun licking her injured paw
and Blackie's brown eyes were fixed longingly on
his new friend. *Why won't you come and play?* he
seemed to be asking.

Adam Hope appeared in his dressing gown.
'So!' he said. 'You've managed to spoil my fine
handiwork have you, young lady?'

Goldie's tail twitched in a hesitant greeting.
She sat down and looked up at Mr Hope with a
sheepish expression.

He bent over her and gently lifted her paw.
'Yep,' he said cheerfully. 'You've made short work
of that lot of stitches. What are we going to do with
you?' Goldie thumped her tail on the floor.

Emily Hope came downstairs and had a look at Goldie's paw, too. Peering over her parents' shoulders, Mandy could see a little dried blood on the fur where the wound had been bleeding again.

'Can't we just bandage it up?' asked James.

Mrs Hope shook her head. 'The wound is gaping a bit, James. It'll need to be stitched again.'

'But she'll only rip them out!' Mandy said.

'You could be right about that.' Adam Hope shook his head. He soothed the Labrador with his hand. 'And we haven't got a cone with us . . .'

'What's a cone?' asked James, who had both arms round Blackie's chest as the black Labrador strained to get closer to Goldie.

'You know, James,' said Mandy. 'It looks like an upturned bucket. Dogs wear it like a collar so they can't lick the places they shouldn't.'

'Oh, yes,' James nodded. 'Did you say you haven't got one, Mr Hope?' He sounded doubtful. Mandy's dad always travelled with his vet's bag, which was stuffed with a never-ending supply of veterinary bits and pieces for any emergency.

'It's not the sort of thing I carry around with me, I'm afraid,' Mr Hope admitted, smiling.

'A lampshade!' Mandy said loudly, making Goldie lift her head and prick up her ears.

James stared at her. 'Yes?' he prompted.

'I spotted one on a shelf in the cupboard in my bedroom! We could use that, couldn't we?' Mandy was delighted with her suggestion.

'Well, at a push . . .' Emily Hope looked doubtful as she filled the kettle. 'We'll have to replace it, of course.'

'Oh, Mum, we will,' Mandy said earnestly. 'I'm sure the owners of the cottage wouldn't mind, not if they knew how important it is.'

'In your cupboard? I'll go and get it,' said James, getting up and pulling Blackie with him.

Goldie put her head down again and sighed. Her foot was clearly causing her some discomfort because she seemed reluctant to move about. Mandy stroked her until James reappeared, holding a battered-looking but sturdy cardboard lampshade. It was bright pink, with a loud floral pattern.

Adam Hope looked up. 'Hmm,' he said. 'You know, I think that in terms of size and fit, this will do the job perfectly! We'll have to cut it open, then fold it round her neck so that it fits snugly.'

'I'm so glad,' said Mandy. She took the shade from James. 'It doesn't weigh much, so it won't be too uncomfortable for her to wear. Dad, what can James and I do to help?'

'Well, you and mum and James can start by magically turning this lampshade into a cone to fit over Goldie's head. I'll sedate her and stitch her up all over again,' said Mr Hope. 'But first, I'll drink a drop of my tea.'

'I'll take Blackie out for a bit,' said James. 'Should I look in the garage for something to cut the lampshade open?'

'Thanks, James,' Mrs Hope smiled. 'That would be a great help. Strangely enough, I haven't brought any pruning shears with me!'

Mandy helped her father prepare the kitchen table for Goldie's second operation. She found a newspaper and spread it out, then set out a pile of sterile wipes and some cotton wool. Meanwhile Adam Hope went to fetch his toolbox from the car.

'You're a great assistant,' said Emily Hope, handing Mandy a mug of hot chocolate.

'Look what I found!' James shot through the kitchen door, tugged along by Blackie. 'It's a hacksaw. It was lying on a shelf in the garage.'

James blew and dust flew off the small saw in all directions.

Mandy sneezed. 'Great!' she said. 'Let's cut up the lampshade.'

'I'll make the first hole, shall I?' suggested Mrs Hope, picking up a kitchen knife. She eased the sharp point of the knife through the cardboard. It gave easily, and she waggled the knife to widen the hole. When it was large enough, James took over with the hacksaw, pushing it back and forth to saw a clean line from top to bottom.

'Neat!' Mandy said approvingly. 'What's next?'

'This is my bit,' said Mr Hope, brandishing a screwdriver he'd retrieved from the toolbox. He turned on a ring of the gas cooker. James and Mandy watched with interest as he held the tip of the metal screwdriver in the flame, turning it until it was glowing white-hot. Even Blackie seemed interested, and stopped straining on his lead to reach Goldie.

Mandy held the lampshade at the wider end as her father instructed. He pressed the scalding screwdriver against the patterned cardboard. There was a sizzling sound and the sharp smell of burning. 'One small hole,' Adam Hope grinned. 'And now another . . .'

'But what're they for?' asked James.

'I'm going to thread some cloth bandage through each of the four holes and tie the lampshade to her collar,' he explained.

James looked puzzled. 'Goldie hasn't got a collar,' he pointed out.

'Not just now she hasn't,' Mr Hope smiled. 'Goldie will have to borrow Blackie's collar, if you don't mind, James?'

'Oh,' said James, adding, 'No, not at all.'

'We can buy Blackie another collar tomorrow morning,' Emily Hope told him. She and Mandy began to cut strips of bandage to thread into the holes round the edge of the lampshade.

'What a great cone,' Mandy declared, delighted with their team effort. At their feet, Goldie was steadily licking her wounded paw, reminding Mandy that the little Labrador still had another operation to face.

'Poor girl,' she said, bending down to stroke her. 'It'll soon be over.'

Emily Hope filled a syringe with sedative. As she approached, the dog flopped her head down with a big sigh, as though she knew exactly what to expect.

* * *

When it was all over, Goldie lay on the floor, sleeping off her sedative.

'Let's pop the lampshade on her now,' suggested Emily Hope. 'She's sleepy enough not to mind.'

Mandy went over to the dog and helped by holding the Labrador's head in both hands. It lolled in her palms and the weight of it surprised her. Goldie's eyelids drooped as Emily Hope folded the cardboard round Goldie's neck, closing it again into its original cone shape. Mr Hope threaded a strip of bandage through each of the holes and tied it firmly to Blackie's collar, which he had had to make smaller to fit Goldie's neck.

'There!' said Mandy's dad, stepping back to admire his handiwork.

'It looks a bit uncomfortable,' said James uncertainly. 'Not her paw. That lampshade thing, I mean.'

'It's called a cone,' Mandy reminded him. 'And I don't think Goldie will mind it too much. The flowers quite suit her!'

'Dogs get used to these sorts of things very quickly,' Adam Hope added.

Goldie's face was out of view, encased in the upturned lampshade. The weight of her head on

the floor made the cone tilt and from within it came the sound of gentle snoring.

'I'd like to thank my team for their expert help with this morning's veterinary emergency,' announced Adam Hope, raising a glass of orange juice in a toast.

'A pleasure,' said James. He sat down at the kitchen table. 'I think we deserve a big breakfast after that!'

Mrs Hope, who was breaking eggs into a pan of sizzling butter, smiled at him. Blackie squeezed under his chair, ever hopeful for a shower of titbits. He'd temporarily forgotten his interest in Goldie in favour of the smell of food.

There was a loud rapping on the front door. Mr

Hope looked at his watch. 'It's not even nine o'clock yet,' he said, surprised. 'Who could that be?'

'We don't know anyone here,' Mandy pointed out.

Emily Hope went to the door, followed by an eager Blackie. Mandy took a last bite of toast and scurried into the hall to see who it was.

'Hello?' Emily Hope said as she opened the door.

A young man stood on the doorstep. His hands were deep in the pockets of his jacket and he looked rather embarrassed. 'Good morning,' he said. 'I'm really sorry to disturb you so early on a Saturday morning. My name's Ben Sullivan.'

'Yes?' Mrs Hope sounded cautious. 'Can we help you?'

'My wife Sue and I used to live in this cottage,' he explained. 'We had a dog, and she's gone missing. I don't think for a moment she would be here but…'

Mandy's heart skipped a beat. *Goldie! Could this possibly be her owner?*

James appeared beside her. He tugged at her sleeve. 'Hang on a minute. How do we know he's really Goldie's owner?' he whispered anxiously. 'I mean, he might be an imposter . . . a thief, or something.'

'Come in,' Emily Hope was saying. She stepped aside to let the visitor into the sitting room.

Mr Sullivan thanked her. 'Our dog's called Daisy,' he said. 'She's a golden—'

But before he could finish, there was a loud clattering and scrambling noise from the kitchen. The flowery lampshade came crashing through the door, cannoning off the door posts. Inside the cone, Goldie staggered against the wall.

'Daisy!' exclaimed Mr Sullivan. 'Where have you *been*? And what have you done to yourself?' He leaned down to welcome the dog with his arms wide open.

The Labrador tried to lick his face, but the cone made it impossible to reach. Ben Sullivan's fingers sank into Goldie's soft yellow fur as he stroked her, and Mandy's eyes filled with sudden, hot tears.

'She turned up on the lawn with a badly cut leg,' Emily Hope explained. 'My husband and I are both vets. We put a few stitches in her paw.'

'Thanks, that was really kind of you!' Mr Sullivan smiled broadly as he looked up at them.

Mandy glanced at James, a wave of relief washing over her. Goldie was really Daisy, and she had found her owner!

Mrs Hope led Ben Sullivan into the kitchen where Adam Hope was spreading marmalade on a slice of toast. He stood up and put out his hand. 'I can guess who you are,' he smiled, shaking Mr Sullivan's hand. 'Goldie took off out of the kitchen like a rocket when she heard your voice!'

'Daisy, Dad,' Mandy said softly. 'Her name is Daisy.'

Everyone warmly invited Mr Sullivan to stay to breakfast. Emily Hope brought a tray of tea into the sitting room, where Daisy lay with her cone resting on Ben's foot. Blackie had curled up as close to Daisy as he could get, as though sensing his friend would soon be gone.

'We called her Goldie,' Mandy told Ben, as she sat cross-legged on the floor with one hand on Daisy's flank. Ben Sullivan had really friendly eyes, she noticed, and a lot of curly brown hair.

'Sue and I got her when she was just eight weeks old,' he said, smiling. 'She's so much a part of our family. We couldn't bear it when she disappeared.'

'What happened?' James prompted. 'How did she get out?'

'Our property is . . . rather big,' said Ben. 'It isn't exactly fenced. Daisy went off exploring soon after we moved away from here – she's rather independent and she's done it before. This time, she must have forgotten her way home, her *new* home, that is.'

'How long is it since she vanished?' asked Emily Hope.

'Two days.' Ben shook his head. 'We've been frantic. I wish I'd thought to come back to the cottage before now. It seemed like such a long way for Daisy to wander.'

'Where are you living now?' Mandy said. Then she drew in her breath so sharply that Blackie barked. Mr Sullivan had just taken off his light raincoat. On the T-shirt he wore underneath was a face that Mandy recognised instantly. It was the otter cub she'd seen on the poster in the post office window!

Ben looked at her in surprise. 'Our new house is about six miles away,' he said. 'In Lakeside.'

'I knew it!' Mandy leaped to her feet. 'We saw a

poster with that otter on it in the post office window here.'

'Lakeside Otter Sanctuary? That's us,' Ben grinned. 'We've only been going a short while. It's been hard work, but very rewarding.'

'An otter sanctuary?' Mrs Hope opened her green eyes wide with interest.

'Yes,' Ben nodded, looking serious. 'It's been a dream of ours to manage a sanctuary for wildlife ever since we married. It seemed a dream that might just come true when my wife, Sue, inherited some money earlier this year.'

'That's wonderful,' Mandy breathed.

'So we decided to rent out this cottage and bought a piece of land we'd had our eye on for a long time,' Ben finished simply.

'In that case, you and you wife must be our temporary landlords?' said Mr Hope.

'I guess so!' Ben laughed, adding, 'And while I'm here, is everything up to scratch?'

'Great,' Adam Hope confirmed. 'Not that we've had a lot of time to inspect the place.' He pointed at Goldie, smiling. She was lying very quietly now, obviously delighted to be reunited with her owner.

'Is she going to be all right?' Ben asked.

'She's fine,' answered Mr Hope. 'She must have cut her foot on something sharp while she was exploring, that's all. I'll give you a few antibiotics to take with you, just in case she's picked up an infection.'

'You've been so good to her,' Mr Sullivan said, bending down to stroke his dog. 'And whose collar is this? It isn't Daisy's.'

'It's my dog, Blackie's,' James spoke up. 'We lent it to her so we could tie on that cone thing she's wearing,' he explained. 'Mr Hope stitched Daisy up, and she undid the stitches with her teeth. We used a lampshade we found upstairs, as it was an emergency.' He suddenly looked uncomfortable, and glanced at Mandy.

'How inventive!' Ben Sullivan laughed. 'I'll replace Blackie's collar for you. And don't worry about the lampshade. It's an ancient old thing, and I never liked it anyway!'

'Daisy was a great patient,' Mandy said.

'I can't thank you enough,' said Mr Sullivan, finishing his tea. 'I'd better get back to Sue and tell her the good news.' He stood up and pulled on his jacket.

'I'm very relieved you thought to come here,' said Emily Hope.

'So am I!' Ben replied, shaking Adam Hope's hand once again.

Mandy glanced at James. He raised his eyebrows at her and she guessed what he was thinking. Should they ask about the otters?

Before she could say anything, Ben spoke again. 'As a thank you for looking after Daisy, would you like to come out tomorrow and spend the day at the sanctuary with us?'

'Would we?' grinned James.

'We'd love it!' Mandy nodded.

Mr Sullivan delved in his coat pocket and produced a leaflet. 'This will tell you how to find us,' he said. 'We'd love to show you round.'

'That'll be great. Thanks,' said Adam Hope, taking the leaflet.

Mandy got down on her knees and looked into Daisy's eyes. The Labrador blinked sleepily back at her from inside her cone. 'It's time to go home, girl,' Mandy told her, rubbing under her chin. 'Your new home, that is. You don't live here any more, remember?' Daisy licked Mandy's hand.

'We'll miss you,' James said to the golden Labrador. 'Especially Blackie.'

'Bring Blackie tomorrow,' said Ben. 'I'm sure

Daisy would love to see him.'

'Thanks.' Mandy gave Daisy one last pat as the dog got clumsily to her feet and tried to hurry to the front door ahead of Ben. It seemed she was determined not to be left behind. But she misjudged the width of the cone and collided with the door frame with a crash. Confused, she sat down and looked up at Ben for help.

'Oh, there'll be a few lessons to be learned with that thing on your head, Daisy,' said Ben.

Mandy soothed the dog and guided her through the door. 'Poor girl,' she murmured sympathetically. Daisy was a funny sight with the lampshade on her head, but Mandy tried to imagine how difficult it must be for her, not to be able to see exactly where she was going.

Outside, Daisy staggered about, getting in the way of Ben's legs. Whenever she wanted to look out sideways from the cone, she had to turn her whole body and if she wasn't bumping into things with the lampshade, she was treading on people's feet.

'She's not going to let you go without her, that's for sure,' smiled Emily Hope.

Ben Sullivan opened the car door and eased

Daisy up on to the back seat. He waved. 'Thanks again,' he said.

Mandy waved back. 'See you tomorrow!' she called.

Five

It was hard not to keep looking at the big kitchen clock as Adam Hope made pancakes the next morning. Mandy had woken before the others and had sat at the window in her bedroom, looking out at the misty dawn and imagining the otter sanctuary. Time seemed to crawl by.

'Missed!' cried Mr Hope, scooping up a pancake from the floor before Blackie could get there. 'I'm not terribly good at this tossing business. Another one, Mandy?'

'I've had enough, Dad, thank you,' Mandy said.

'I'll have another one, please,' mumbled James,

his mouth full. 'They're really good.'

'It's a lovely day,' remarked Emily Hope, peering out of the window. 'I think we should leave as soon as we can so we don't miss a moment of our day at the sanctuary.'

'I agree!' Mandy got up and took her plate to the sink. James followed, the remains of his second pancake in one hand. He hurried about fetching Blackie's lead and filling an empty plastic bottle with cold water. Mandy scraped a brush through her blonde hair and gathered it into a ponytail, then ran round the cottage looking for her trainers and a bowl for Blackie to drink from. At last, they were ready to leave.

It was an easy drive to Lakeside, along small roads bordered by lush woodland on one side, and a winding river that ran into the lake on the other. Blackie had his nose out of the top half of the window on James's side of the car. His soft furry cheek billowed and flapped as the wind caught it, making Mandy laugh.

Emily Hope navigated from the map on the leaflet Ben Sullivan had given them. 'It says here that the grounds of the sanctuary include two small connected lakes,' she read. 'What a great place for otters. We're nearly there, Adam . . . slow down a bit. We're looking for a turning on the left called Waterhead Lane.'

'Here it is,' said Mr Hope.

The lane was heavily tree-lined. Soon Mandy saw a small metal sign hanging on a broad tree trunk. It featured the silhouette of an otter and an arrow. 'Not far now.' She smiled at James, who was having difficulty trying to keep Blackie from squeezing out of the window.

'It's the smells,' he explained. 'They're different from the ones at home.'

Mandy laughed. 'Maybe he knows he's about to see Daisy again?'

'He must do,' replied James, holding on tightly to Blackie.

Adam Hope slowed the Land-rover to a crawl and Mandy looked out to see a large wooden carving of an otter nailed to one of a pair of white stone pillars. 'We're here!' she announced, snapping off her seatbelt and craning forward to look out.

Adam Hope turned left through the pillars and followed a bumpy track. Just visible through the trees, the morning sun shimmered and bounced off the sparkling surface of a lake. After a kilometre, the track opened out into a tarred, circular forecourt in front of a small whitewashed house.

The first thing Mandy saw was Daisy. The golden Labrador was spread out in the sun, her coat gleaming, but she raised her head and looked at the approaching car. She stood up to give a joyous bark when she saw Blackie's sleek black nose sticking out of the window.

'Hi, Daisy!' Mandy called from her side. Blackie's ears shot up and his tail began to wag hard.

'Welcome!' Ben Sullivan came striding towards them from inside the house. Mandy held on to Blackie while James quickly looped the lead around his dog's collar-less neck. Then they got out of the car to say hello.

'Hi there! Did you have any problem finding us?' asked Ben.

'No problem at all,' said Adam Hope with a smile.

'Can I let Blackie go, Mr Sullivan?' James asked. His dog was quivering and straining forward at the sight of Daisy.

'Sure,' replied Ben. 'Daisy's pretty steady on three legs.' Then he added, 'She's not mad about that thing on her head though!'

Mandy watched as Blackie bounded happily

over to Daisy. Her plumy tail waved back and forth, her injured paw held just off the ground.

'This place is great!' said Mandy. She looked across a sunny expanse of lawn to a wide, fast-moving rush of brown water, hoping for a sign of the resident otters.

'Well, we're a bit off the beaten track here but we've managed to attract a few interested visitors already,' said Ben.

'Good,' said Mrs Hope. 'I'm sure in time you're going to be very busy.'

'Come along in and meet Sue,' said Ben, gesturing to the front door of the house.

Right on cue, Sue Sullivan appeared in the doorway, a huge smile on her face. 'Hello! I'm so glad to have a chance to meet you all, and to thank you for being so kind to Daisy,' she said.

Mr and Mrs Hope stepped into the hall and shook hands with her. 'We were so glad to have been able to help,' Emily Hope told Sue.

Mrs Sullivan's hair was almost the same colour as Mandy's mother's – a chestnut red – and she wore it pulled back into a loose bun. Her cheerful face was freckled and her blue eyes shone when she spoke. Mandy liked her immediately.

'Would you like a tour, then?' asked Ben,

flattening himself against the wall to allow Daisy to get past in her cone. Blackie followed faithfully, his tongue lolling.

'Yes, please,' Mandy said eagerly.

'Maybe you two would like to lend us a hand?' said Sue, looking at James and Mandy in turn. 'There's a lot of work to be done and we could do with some help.'

'We'll do anything,' Mandy promised, and James nodded enthusiastically.

'Anything,' he repeated.

'That's nice to hear! Ben and I have devoted this morning to catching up on paperwork,' Sue explained. 'There's still the lunchtime feeding and cleaning to be done.'

'I'd like to take a look at Daisy's paw,' said Mr Hope and Mrs Hope nodded in agreement. 'We'll catch up with you in a bit.'

'Right,' said Sue, grinning at Mandy and James. 'You two can come and meet our residents.'

Mandy smoothed Daisy's back. 'Make sure Blackie minds his manners, Daisy,' she teased. Blackie was standing nose-to-nose with the golden dog. Only his shoulders and back were visible; his head had vanished into the opening of Daisy's upturned lampshade, and two Labrador tails were wagging like mad. Mandy, James and Sue burst out laughing.

Sue Sullivan's first stop was a brick outbuilding used for storage. She delved into a small refrigerator and filled a bucket with chopped raw fish and earthworms. 'An otter's favourite food,' she announced cheerfully.

'Fish and earthworms?' Mandy said disbelievingly. Fish she could understand, but worms didn't sound very appetising at all!

'Yes – and they love eels, toads and other small mammals. They've got very sharp eyes and sensitive whiskers for finding food in dark, murky places. They use their sharp claws for digging up worms.' She handed James and Mandy two long-handled outdoor brooms. They eagerly followed her outside as she began her rounds.

'You're bound to get mucky,' she warned.

'We don't mind,' James told her.

The smelly contents of the bucket slopped from side to side as Sue Sullivan strode along, heading for the river.

Mandy took a deep breath to contain her excitement. She was about to meet the otters of Lakeside at last.

As they drew closer to the riverbank, she heard a merry, high-pitched chattering sound. It came from the direction of a stream that bubbled through the undergrowth before joining the main river.

'Otters like to live in dank places, in the river bank or in reed beds, so Ben and I have built the enclosures as close to the water as possible,' Sue explained. 'We've tried to imitate their natural environment.'

They had arrived at a pen enclosed with waist-high wire mesh. The fence extended into the river, so that the water flowed right through the pen. Sue opened the gate and ushered Mandy and James in ahead of her. Mandy stood still, searching the piles of logs, stones and plants for the otter. Under a stack of leafy branches, a pair of beady bright eyes peeped out at her. Mandy slowly walked forward, following Sue's lead, and went down on her haunches when she was close enough to the animal to touch it. Mandy was hardly breathing, afraid that the otter would scamper away and hide, but she couldn't have been more wrong.

The otter reared up on its hind legs less than a metre away from her, resting two webbed front feet on a round tummy. He chattered loudly at Sue, and she laughed. 'This is Jinx,' she said. 'He was the first otter to come to the sanctuary.'

She reached into her bucket and tossed Jinx a bit of fish. James and Mandy watched, spellbound, as the otter dropped on to all fours and waddled on large webbed feet to snatch up the fish hungrily. His furry body was just over a metre long, ending in a powerful, tapered tail.

'Oh, he's beautiful,' Mandy breathed. The otter's coat was a baggy swathe of brown velvet that

almost looked too big for the small animal inside. On either side of its broad muzzle was a set of transparent whiskers.

'Chirp,' said Jinx, looking longingly at Sue. She threw a second chunk of fish and it landed in the water flowing through the pen. The otter splashed into the water after it, snatched it up, than rolled on to his back. Holding the fish on his chest, clasped between his two webbed feet, he began to crunch happily.

'Oh, he's magic!' Mandy said softly.

'It looks a little bit like a koala bear,' James decided. 'But even more cute.'

'Well, perhaps his nose does,' agreed Sue. 'But that's where the similarity ends. Otters are as quick as lightning, and amazingly dexterous with their hands. They can also be very fierce. They may look cute and cuddly but they're carnivores who can bite and scratch like giant cats.'

'Why is Jinx in the sanctuary. Is he ill?' asked Mandy, who couldn't take her eyes off the animal.

'He's a lot better than he was when we found him,' said Sue. 'He'd swallowed a fishing hook and was slowly starving to death.'

Mandy looked at the eager little face gobbling

up the fish. The furry brown tummy poking above the water looked full to bursting. 'Not any more!' she laughed. 'He's as plump as anything.'

'Well, he needs a thick layer of fat under his furry coat to keep him warm. Otters love to swim and play in water. They're what we call semi-aquatic because they spend so much of their life in water. They can hold their breath underwater for up to four minutes.'

Suddenly Jinx stiffened. He rolled over and pulled himself out of the water. Then he sat up and clasped his front paws together over his chest, looking from side to side with great interest. Mandy turned round to see what had caught Jinx's attention. The two Labradors had appeared some distance away. Blackie spotted James and broke into a run, leaving Daisy limping behind.

James gasped. 'Blackie!' he said, going red. 'I hope he won't frighten Jinx.'

Sue shook her head. 'Jinx is pretty used to Daisy being around,' she reassured him.

The black Labrador came bounding over to James with an aren't-you-pleased-to-see-me look on his face. He seemed delighted to have found everyone. Then he spotted Jinx. Blackie's ears shot up and he cocked his head.

Mandy made a grab for him but Blackie wasn't wearing a collar. Quick as a flash, he slipped in through the unfastened gate.

'No!' cried James, lunging for his dog and missing. Blackie crouched down on the edge of the river, his chest and stomach soaking up the watery mud, and stared at the otter as though he couldn't believe his eyes. Jinx gave a warning cry, a high-pitched squeal that startled Mandy. She saw the otter's razor-sharp teeth.

The squeal startled Blackie, too. He scrambled to his paws and scooted behind James's legs.

'Blackie!' James said sternly, bright red with embarrassment. 'Bad, bad dog!' Blackie's ears went down and he slunk back out of the gate, where he stood looking through the wire, wagging his tail hopefully.

'Don't worry,' said Sue. 'There's no harm done. Jinx doesn't seem too bothered and, as you can see, otters can be just as fierce as dogs!'

Daisy padded up to join them. She was still trying to dislodge the uncomfortable lampshade. She sat down and scratched noisily at the rim.

Sue petted her. 'Let's move on. There are more otters for you to meet.'

'How many otters do you have at the moment?' Mandy asked, as she closed the gate.

'Eleven altogether,' replied Sue.

'How do you get them?' James wondered, using the handle of his broom as a walking stick, so that he left a trail of neat round dents next to his footprints.

'Well, we haven't been open very long, but our reputation is quickly spreading so sometimes people bring the otters to us,' explained Sue.

'Are most of them wounded?' Mandy asked.

Sue nodded sadly. 'Many of them are injured crossing roads at night, although some are just sickly. Our aim is to nurse them back to good health, then release them back into the wild.'

'It's a very good idea,' said James.

'Where do they live, in the wild?' said Mandy, bending down to smoothe Blackie's coat as he walked beside her.

'They dig out dens, called holts, in the banks of rivers, mainly,' Sue answered. 'Or they will take over an abandoned den dug by some other animal. Sometimes they make their holts among the roots of trees.'

'Oh, look,' said Mandy, pointing.

They had arrived at another pen. This one was set back from the river, so it had a man-made pool in the centre. Around the pool were three large hollow logs, and on one of the logs sat two little otters.

'We've put two young male otters together in here – Otto and Splash,' Sue told them. 'Ben and I thought we might one day need to use this pen as a kind of isolation unit, if we ever had an otter with an infectious disease.'

'They're much smaller than Jinx,' Mandy observed. She hung over the gate, smiling at the lovable little faces that looked back at her with great curiosity. 'Why are they here?'

'They were found huddled together when a stretch of riverbank was being cleared for development,' said Sue. 'The bank collapsed under the weight of the earthmoving machines. We were just lucky that one of the drivers spotted the otters in time.'

'Thankfully!' Mandy sighed.

'Go inside,' urged Sue, unlatching the gate. 'Could you help me by washing and brushing out their pool?'

'We'd love to!' Mandy was thrilled. She stepped through the gate.

'James, there's a hosepipe in the corner over there. See it?' Sue pointed. 'You can use that to sluice out the pool.'

'Yep.' James hurried off.

'Great. Thanks, you two. I'm off to feed the others. I'll come back in a bit,' Sue said.

Otto and Splash didn't seem to mind Mandy and James working in their pen. They scurried inside a big, hollowed-out log at first, but soon popped out of the other end, their natural curiosity getting the better of them. Splash began to amble around like a small brown seal, getting in the way of Mandy's stream of water and rolling on his back to clap his paws in the spray. Mandy was enchanted. The otter made happy little noises that sounded like 'hah!' and she felt as though he was laughing with her.

'He's amazing!' she breathed. 'Look, James, he wants me to wash his tummy!'

Blackie had a chastened expression on his face as he watched them from the shade of a tree. Daisy lay nearby, resting her chin on the underside of her cone and dozing in the warm sun.

When Sue came over to see how Mandy and James were getting on, the bucket she carried had been refilled. She poured out a pile of fish. Mandy watched as Otto emerged from the log to eat, holding a piece of fish in both paws.

'They're lovely,' James said softly.

'They look so *well* now,' Mandy agreed.

'Yes, it won't be long before they can go free,' Sue told them. 'We'll let them loose downriver.' Then she added, 'You've done a great job here. Come and meet Sprite now.'

As Mandy latched the gate and turned to follow Sue, she noticed that Otto and Splash had come up to the fence behind her and were peering out through the wire. They stood on their hind legs, holding on to the mesh with their sharp front claws. Mandy was glad to know they would soon be back in the river.

James whistled for Blackie. The Labrador's tail was waving merrily again, as though he was happy that James had forgiven him, but he cast a wary glance over his shoulder at the otters as he went past the pen. Daisy limped behind him, looking demure and disinterested in the otters.

'Daisy was bitten by an otter not so long ago,' Sue explained. 'It taught her to be a lot more careful around them!'

When they arrived at the next enclosure, Mandy saw that the resident otter was shaggy-coated and considerably larger than Otto and Splash.

'This is our Sprite,' said Sue. 'He's not a very happy chap, I'm afraid.'

The otter lay on his back, his mouth open to show a row of sharp little teeth, holding one bandaged paw against his chest. His muzzle was silvery grey and crusted with dried mud. When Sue, James and Mandy stopped to look at him, he didn't move a muscle, although his eyes were open.

'What's wrong with him?' Mandy whispered.

'Poor Sprite lost his mate in an accident,' explained Sue. 'A car collided with the pair a few weeks ago. He fractured a couple of his ribs and tore off a claw. Sadly, his mate was killed.'

'Oh, dear!' Mandy said sadly.

'That's awful,' agreed James.

Sue nodded. 'Even though his ribs have mended, he seems lonely and a bit depressed,' she told them. 'Otters are very clean animals and Sprite hasn't groomed himself once since he arrived. He's not keen on his food either. We're quite worried about him.'

Sprite regarded the visitors from his upside-down viewpoint without a flicker of real interest. Mandy was struck by the contrast in moods between Sprite and the other, playful otters. As she watched, he scratched lazily at his grey tummy with his good paw.

'It must sometimes make you sad, working here,' said James.

'It is awful when the animals are found struggling to survive – but it's also very rewarding,' replied Sue. 'Our job is to heal them and set them free to breed in the wild. In some parts of the world, otters are on the endangered animal list. We're trying to change all that.'

'That's great,' Mandy said approvingly.

'Let's go back to the house now.' Sue looked at her watch. 'I've saved the best till last!'

James's eyebrows shot up expectantly. 'What's that?' he asked.

'Cubs!' Sue grinned. 'Orphaned otter cubs, just a few weeks old.'

'Oh, how fantastic!' Mandy breathed.

'I've got to mix up some formula for their bottle.

I'm sure you'd like to help me feed them, wouldn't you?'

Before Mandy could reply, there came a shout. Sue looked over towards the house. It was Ben, and he was calling her name urgently and waving his arms.

'Oh!' she said. 'Something must have happened!' She began to run.

Mandy and James exchanged a glance, then began to sprint after Sue, with Blackie in hot pursuit. Daisy was left behind, her lampshade bobbing as she limped hurriedly over the grass.

They arrived back at the house in time to see Ben gently take an otter from the arms of a woman. Mandy's mum and dad stood nearby, watching anxiously. A car was parked at an awkward angle in front of the house and the driver's door was open.

'I didn't see it,' the woman said tearfully. 'It just stepped out in front of my car . . . it was too late not to hit it. I'm so sorry!'

Sue put an arm round the woman's shoulders. 'It was good of you to bring it to us,' she said kindly. 'We'll do our best.' Then she turned and hurried round the side of the house after Ben and Mandy's parents.

Mandy and James looked at one another in horror. The sight of the otter lying limply in Ben's arms had been a huge shock. How badly had the little animal been hurt?

Six

Mandy, James and Blackie were right behind Ben, Sue and Mandy's mum and dad as they rushed the otter into an outbuilding at the far side of a yard behind the house. It was an old dairy that had been turned into a treatment room and residential unit for sick otters. It was cool and clean, with whitewashed walls and a few rusty milk churns still standing along the wall under the window.

James firmly closed the door on a curious Blackie. Mandy watched the otter being lowered gently on to a shiny metal table. She squeezed in among the four adults, making room at the table for James. The otter's eyes were closed and Mandy's heart speeded up with dread. Was the poor creature still alive?

She was reassured when Ben spoke. 'She's pretty well stunned, but not fully unconscious.' He turned to Adam and Emily Hope. 'What a good thing you two happened to be here! Will you take a look?'

Emily Hope had found a roll of cloth bandage on a shelf with other medical supplies. 'She's docile enough not to need sedating, but we should be cautious and muzzle her, in case she suddenly wakes up,' she suggested.

Adam Hope agreed. He held the otter while Mandy's mum tied a strip of the bandage around the otter's triangular-shaped black nose. Mandy had a glimpse of very powerful-looking teeth as the otter gave a small shudder and her lip curled for a moment. Gently, she was rolled on to her back to be examined for injuries. Mr Hope flexed each webbed paw, feeling for possible breaks in the bones.

'Are her ribs intact?' asked Sue.

'Seem to be,' replied Mr Hope, frowning as he concentrated on feeling the otter's spine.

Mandy felt a pang of worry. The otter looked so trusting and so peaceful lying there. She loved its small, cup-shaped ears. She was longing to reach out and sink her fingers into the thick, fawn-coloured fur on its head, both to offer comfort and to feel its softness. She watched the rise and fall of the animal's laboured breathing. The otter's eyelids flickered, but she seemed unaware of the probing human fingers on her body.

'She'll be OK, won't she?' Mandy asked quietly.

Sue Sullivan slipped a friendly arm round Mandy's shoulders. 'I'm sure she will. Female otters are always the fighters, in my experience.'

'And there's no blood,' added James. 'That's a good thing.'

'You're right, James. There isn't a wound, and she hasn't broken any bones,' said Mandy's dad. He lifted each of the otter's eyelids in turn. Mandy watched carefully, and thought she could see signs of injury around one of the eyeballs.

Her dad confirmed it. 'Ah, here's our problem. The eye is swollen and has some blood in it. That's where she took the blow from the car.'

'She's probably suffering from concussion,' said Emily Hope.

'Is she going to be blind?' asked James.

'I don't think so,' said Mrs Hope. 'She's had a very hard blow to her head and her brain is probably a bit inflamed. I expect she has a horrible headache, but she'll mend in time.'

'She'll need to be kept quiet, preferably in a darkened place,' Mr Hope suggested.

'That's no problem. We've got a room set aside that will do,' Sue spoke up.

'I'll go and prepare a holding cage,' Ben offered, 'and see if I can darken the room somehow.'

'Thanks, Ben,' said Emily Hope.

'I'll come with you,' said Sue.

'Why does it have to be dark?' James looked puzzled.

'Her eye is damaged, so looking into the bright light won't help her,' Mr Hope explained. He slipped a needle into the soft skin at the back of the otter's furry neck, then massaged it with his fingers to help speed the drug into the bloodstream.

Mandy felt relieved. It looked like the otter had had a lucky escape. While her parents talked about the sort of drug they would give the otter, she put a gentle hand on the thick brown fur. 'Oh, James,' she whispered. 'She's so soft!'

As James stroked the otter, her mouth opened and closed with a soft, smacking sound. James jumped back and quickly withdrew his hand.

'Shall we give her a name?' Mandy whispered.

'D'you think Sue and Ben would mind?' wondered James.

'Shouldn't think so. What about Belle? It's a lovely name for a lady otter!' Mandy suggested.

'It's French for beautiful,' James pointed out. 'You're right. It seems to suit her.'

'Belle,' Mandy said, when Sue rejoined them. 'James and I want to call the otter Belle. Is that all right?'

Sue smiled. 'She'll need a name if she's going to stay with us while she recovers. And Belle is a fine name.'

Belle's little head lolled as Adam Hope carried her behind Sue to a small room next to the dairy. There he lowered the otter gently into a cage that stood on a table in the middle of the room. Sue had spread an old quilt inside the cage, and Mandy thought it looked very comfortable. Belle lay on her side, with her eyes closed, and gave a big sigh.

'She'll be fine in a few days,' Sue said happily.

'That's great news,' Mandy smiled.

'Now, as she seems to be sleeping off her ordeal quite comfortably, why don't we have some lunch?'

James looked interested. 'That sounds like a very good idea,' he nodded.

After lunch, Sue got ready to take James and Mandy to see the otter cubs. Ben found a bone for Blackie and the dog carried it off proudly, his tail wagging, to a corner of the front garden where he could enjoy it undisturbed. Daisy stayed indoors, resting under the kitchen table on the cool, stone floor.

Mandy had been waiting patiently to see the cubs throughout the meal, and now she was almost bursting with excitement. 'How old are they?' she puffed, jogging to keep up with Sue as she headed for the building where they were housed.

'Just a month or so,' Sue replied, shaking up some milk formula in a large bottle as she walked. 'We don't know what happened to the mother. The cubs were found on a riverbank by a bird watcher, mewing for attention like kittens.'

'Maybe she died,' James mused sadly. 'The mother, I mean.'

'It's quite likely,' Sue agreed. 'Otters are usually very good, protective parents. The mother takes care of the cubs for about a year, and the father joins the family to help with feeding and training when she takes them out of the den.'

The cubs were in an old pigsty in a walled yard at the back of the dairy. As they approached the door, Mandy heard the otters calling faintly.

'They're hungry,' said Sue, adding, 'Again!'

Mandy and James peeped over a waist-high stone wall. There was a large cardboard box on the concrete floor of the yard. Inside the box, the cubs were curled up together in a bed of straw. Their eyes were closed, so that it was difficult to tell where one sleek, dark brown body ended and the next began. Then, one of the cubs opened a hazy little eye.

'Wow!' breathed James. 'They're so small.'

'Aren't they adorable!' Mandy whispered. She could have fitted a cub in each of her hands. They had funny flat faces and small pink mouths, which they opened wide to call loudly until Sue lowered the teat of the bottle into the box. The cubs' tiny noses began to twitch with interest. They slithered apart, raising their faces eagerly for the milk they could smell, making earnest chirping noises like baby birds in a nest. Mandy saw tiny, needle-like teeth as one cub latched on and began to suck. It made Mandy smile to see how eagerly the cub paddled its front feet, its throat working as it swallowed the milk. The second cub had opened its eyes and gave a determined bark.

'All right, all right,' laughed Sue. 'Your turn next.'

'Have they got names?' asked James.

'This is Leo. The female is Eva,' Sue told them, pointing to each cub in turn. 'They're utterly gorgeous, aren't they? I try to handle them as little as possible, hard though it is. I prefer them not to carry the scent of humans when they are released back into the river.'

'Just like that?' Mandy said, not taking her eyes off the otters. 'As soon as they're bigger, you'll be able to let them go off on their own?' It was Eva's turn to drink, and she had a tide of milky froth round her mouth.

'Not exactly,' Sue explained. 'I plan to introduce them into the special holt Ben and I are building downriver. It's not an enclosure but a proper open habitat, so they have free access to the river.'

'That's wonderful,' Mandy said enthusiastically. She looked down into the box again. The male cub's tummy was swollen with warm milk. He curled up in the straw and rolled on to his back. His eyes closed again and opened only for a second when Eva joined him. She settled herself across his belly, stretched out and yawned, then fell asleep.

When Sue went back to the house to wash the bottle, Mandy and James took the chance to wander round the sanctuary again.

'What a great place,' said James.

'We're really lucky to have it so close to our holiday cottage,' Mandy remarked.

'It was meeting Daisy that led us here,' James reminded her. 'Without her, we might have missed that poster in the post office and we wouldn't have known about the sanctuary.'

Mandy nodded. They'd arrived at Sprite's enclosure, the otter Mandy felt most concerned about. 'He's the sad one,' she recalled. 'The others have injuries that will get better, but this one has a broken heart.'

'He misses his mate,' James agreed.

Sprite lay perfectly still, his eyes blank. The food Sue had put down for him earlier had begun to smell strongly of rancid fish. As Mandy and James sat watching him, there was a gleeful bark and Blackie came tearing through the trees. He skidded to a stop when he saw them, sending up a shower of dirt and twigs. Still, Sprite didn't move.

'Blackie!' scolded James, brushing sand off his trousers. He pushed his glasses up on his nose. 'Calm down, will you?'

'I see a wobbling lampshade,' Mandy smiled, pointing.

Daisy limped towards them, followed by Ben. In her owner's hand was a large metal toolbox. 'Want to come with me downriver to see the holt we're building?' he asked.

'Yes, please!' Mandy answered. 'We were trying to cheer up Sprite.'

'He does seem unhappy, doesn't he?' Ben frowned. 'He needs another mate, a female otter of the right temperament and age. I'm sure the right companion would bring a spark to Sprite's eye!'

He led them along a trail beside the river. The clear water sparkled in the sunlight. Daisy tried to drink, but her mouth was well short of the lip of the lampshade, and she couldn't reach. Blackie paddled at the edge, churning the mud with his big paws, but he seemed much quieter today, as though he was trying to show off his good manners.

'Daisy is setting Blackie a good example,' remarked James. 'Look how well he's behaving!'

'He's having a perfect day,' Mandy said. 'It's turning out to be just one long walk, and he's got his new best friend with him.'

Ahead of them, Ben had slowed down and was crouching on his heels.

Mandy hurried over. She saw a large, level platform made of logs, flush with the ground ahead of them. Underneath it was a kind of den, dug into the bank and going back about a metre. She and James stood at the edge of the platform and looked down into the hole.

'Is this the river holt?' she asked.

'Yes,' replied Ben. 'This is it. All our own design and handiwork.' He stepped down on to the edge of the river. 'It's called a pipe-and-chamber holt,' he told them. 'It's a safe resting place for passing otters and a great start for our own sanctuary otters. Want to take a look?'

James and Mandy jumped down beside him and peered inside. The holt was criss-crossed with a number of long round pipes lying on the muddy floor. They were just wide enough for an otter to squeeze into. The ground underfoot was squelchy with mud and rivulets of water kept trickling in from the sides of the bank.

'I'm glad I'm not an otter,' muttered James,

peering into a long, dark pipe. 'I don't think I'd like to sleep in there.'

Above them, Blackie was sniffing at the log roof and Mandy saw him put out a tentative paw to scrape at something lodged underneath. Then he slithered down the bank to investigate the opening to the den.

Ben looked up. 'Those logs are not secure yet. I'm going to rope them together and nail them today.'

'We'll help,' Mandy said eagerly.

'There's isn't much more to do,' Ben said. 'It's a pretty fine holt the way it is but I want to make it safe. It would be awful if somebody fell though the logs into a muddy pit of metal pipes!'

'Awful for the otters, too,' Mandy agreed.

'Too right! Sprite will be our first resident here, I think. We'll transfer him as soon as he starts to eat.'

'Maybe he *will* eat when he's here,' suggested James. 'Maybe he likes toads or voles or water rats better than the fish you give him?'

'Oh, we've tried him on all kinds of delicious things,' Ben smiled. 'He's hardly eating enough of anything to keep himself alive just now.'

'How sad,' Mandy said, feeling very sorry for the

bereaved otter. 'He must have loved his mate very much.'

Daisy stood on the bank beside the holt, looking down at the gathering at the shoreline of the river. She gave an impatient shake of her head, and the lampshade jiggled against her collar. Blackie scrabbled back up the bank and shot over to where she stood, barking joyously.

He began to tear around in circles, trying to encourage his friend to join in a game. Daisy started to bounce along beside him, at a more ladylike pace. She held her sore paw off the ground and hurried as best she could after Blackie as he sprinted on to the log roof of the holt.

'Hey, you two . . .' Ben began. 'Easy now . . .'

But it was too late. Blackie had come crashing across the makeshift roof. As his paws pounded against the logs they began to roll, and Blackie panicked. He scrabbled, frantically trying to find his footing. With an ominous rumble, the logs toppled down. The last Mandy saw of Blackie was his startled face as the roof caved in and he fell with an anguished howl into the den below.

Seven

'Oh, no!' Mandy gasped.

She dropped quickly to her knees and began to crawl forward into the den. She could just see Blackie among a pile of pipes and sand. He seemed dazed. Mandy tugged at the heavy pipes and dug at the mud with her hands to free his legs.

'Is he all right?' James called anxiously. There wasn't enough room for him to join Mandy inside the holt.

'He's fine . . . I think,' she reported over her shoulder. Just then, a surprised Blackie scrabbled to his feet, scattering earth in all directions. 'Yes,' she said, 'he is fine, James.'

Blackie gave a tremendous shake, then skittered out to the edge of the river, where James and Ben stood doubled over and staring into the holt. The dog's tail was tucked tightly between his legs. Mandy crept out of the den and stood up.

'Thanks, Mandy,' said James. His face was pink with shame. 'Oh, I'm so sorry, Mr Sullivan,' he whispered. He shook his head from side to side, looking, for a moment, as though he would like to crawl into the holt and disappear.

Mandy touched James's shoulder. 'Blackie's not hurt,' she said. 'So that's good, at least.'

'Well!' said Ben Sullivan, trying to sound cheerful. 'That's made short work of that project.' He grinned ruefully at James.

Mandy surveyed the damage. The carefully arranged network of piping was in ruins. The wooden roof had completely caved in, with only a single pole still lying neatly at ground level. Mandy was standing at the edge of nothing more than a heap of beams and pipes, wedged in wet sand.

Daisy appeared on the bank, and stood looking sheepishly down at them. She cocked her head enquiringly at Blackie, and the flowered lampshade tilted comically to one side, but Blackie sat down beside James and refused to look at her.

'I hope you're ashamed,' James told his dog. He had mud in one eye and had to take off his glasses to rub at it.

'Well, I think Daisy egged him on,' said Ben. 'The pair of them were going crazy up there.'

Mandy could see he was bitterly disappointed. This holt was Sue's pride and joy – and it was meant to be ready to receive the otters that were well enough to return to the wild. 'We'll rebuild it for you, Mr Sullivan,' she offered. 'James and I will put it back just the way it was.'

He shook his head. 'That's kind of you, Mandy. But it'll take some time.'

'Well, we're here for a week!' James sounded determined.

'And I'm sure my mum and dad would help,' Mandy added.

Ben smiled at them. 'Well, Sue and I do have a lot of work on up at the sanctuary just now, so maybe . . .'

'Thanks, Mr Sullivan,' said James. 'We'd really like to make up for everything.'

'OK, OK.' Ben laughed and held up his hands. 'Let's go up to the house and tell the others what's happened. I need a cup of tea – and then we'll make a plan.'

'It's not your fault!' Sue Sullivan told James, handing him a glass of iced lemonade. 'Please don't feel bad about it.'

They were sitting in the kitchen, round a table cluttered with a computer, piles of stationery and black files bulging with paperwork. Blackie was lying under the table looking subdued.

'Blackie was just being high-spirited,' said Emily Hope. 'He's mad about Daisy. Perhaps he was trying to impress her.'

Daisy put her good front paw on to Sue's lap. Sue smoothed the dog's head lovingly. Then she looked up at Mr and Mrs Hope, James and Mandy. 'Well, thanks to your kind offer of help, we might still have the river holt ready in time for our conservation grant.'

'What's this?' Adam Hope looked interested.

'We should be awarded a grant by the local council if we develop this as a wildlife conservation site,' explained Ben. 'We're due to be inspected next week.'

'Oh!' said Mandy, putting her drink down with such force that the ice cubes rattled. 'Then we'd better start work right away!'

'Of course. We'll all help,' said Emily Hope.

'I'm in,' added Mr Hope.

'You've been terrific, all of you,' Ben grinned. 'It was a lucky day that our Daisy chose you to come to for help!'

Mandy glanced at James. She could tell he was thinking the same thing as her – if it wasn't for them, the holt would still be in one piece.

Emily Hope looked at her watch. 'It's getting late,' she said. 'Perhaps we should drive home now, and report for duty first thing in the morning?'

Mandy's father stood up. 'That's good thinking,' he said approvingly. 'We'll come back tomorrow, bright and early.'

'Thanks,' Ben grinned. 'We really appreciate it.'

Mandy was reluctant to leave. She kissed Daisy on the top of her head, then slipped out to the treatment room to take another look at Belle. The otter had woken up and her eyes were wide open. She lay on her quilt looking around her. When Mandy approached she buried her head in the folds and tried to hide.

'Belle,' Mandy whispered, kneeling down so she could get as close to the otter as possible. 'I won't hurt you. I hope you feel better. I'll be back to see you tomorrow.'

Belle shifted about in her bedding and Mandy saw the top of her furry head emerge. Two solemn brown eyes stared back at her in the gloom of the darkened room. 'Please get well,' said Mandy, wishing she could cuddle the otter in her arms. 'Please!'

The next day, Emily and Adam Hope debated whether to leave Blackie at Laurel Cottage or take

him to the sanctuary. Blackie had sensed a trip out was on the cards. He wagged his tail as hard as he could and finally won over Mrs Hope by presenting her with his lead. He held it in his mouth with his most appealing expression.

'We can't leave him!' chuckled Mandy's mum. 'He's such a softie. Look at him!'

'He would be very unhappy if he was left behind,' James put in.

'That's settled then.' Mandy was pleased. Blackie could sometimes be a bit of a nuisance, but he was a lovable nuisance and a great friend.

Adam Hope had packed the car with their wellington boots and added a spade he'd found in the garage. They'd put together a picnic lunch, found an assortment of sun hats and were ready to leave by nine.

Mandy stuck her head out of the Land-rover window as they drove along. It was another lovely day and through the trees she could see bright white sails out on the lake. She was longing to see Belle and the other otters, and wondered if Sue would allow her to feed the cubs again.

The car lurched up the long, bumpy driveway of the otter sanctuary. Daisy pricked up her ears when they pulled up outside the cottage and walked gingerly over to meet them, wagging her tail in greeting. Mandy noticed that she was just allowing her injured foot to touch the ground. Definitely a limp rather than a hop, she thought with satisfaction. Spotting her, Blackie whimpered in excitement.

'Daisy's looking much better now,' observed Adam Hope, as if reading Mandy's thoughts. 'It's almost time to think about removing her cone.'

Neither Ben nor Sue seemed to be about so Emily Hope suggested they make their way down to the holt and get to work.

'You be a good boy today,' James told Blackie, as he pulled on his wellingtons. 'And get your nose out of that picnic!' He grabbed Blackie and tugged him away from the basket.

'I'll carry that,' said Mr Hope, scooping the hamper away from the Labrador's muzzle.

'I'll lead the way,' said Mandy.

They walked in single file along the well-trodden path to where the river widened.

'Oh dear,' said Mrs Hope, when she saw the mess Blackie had made of the holt. 'He really did wreck it, didn't he?'

James and Mr Hope began by hauling the logs, one by one, out of the sand. The logs were as heavy as they looked and James was perspiring by the time they'd finished. Mandy was glad of her parents' help. She and James would never have managed alone. While her dad and James dealt with the logs, she and her mum fished out all of the separate pieces of piping and dragged them up on to the bank. Then they were faced with rebuilding the gaping, three-sided excavation. The river washed in at the entrance where the sand had crumbled, making the ground even squelchier.

Blackie took the chance to cool off in the river. He lay on his tummy in the shallow water, until he was startled by a large fish.

'Look!' yelled James, pointing. 'It jumped right out of the water.'

'How nice that the otters will have their meals right on their new doorstep,' Mandy chuckled.

'Frogs, fish, water snails and insects galore. What a feast!' Emily Hope called over her shoulder. She was on all fours in the muddy depths of the holt. Mandy was passing segments of metal pipe to her. Mrs Hope laid them in grooves she had dug into the soil with her trowel to make sure they wouldn't roll away.

'Hello!'

Mandy looked up and saw Sue and Ben standing up on the bank

'You've done wonders already!' remarked Sue.

'Thanks!' said Mandy. 'It's like working in a giant sandpit!'

Above her, James and her dad had already rebuilt part of the roof, placing the logs side by side across the top of the pit. Their hands and knees were muddy and their faces red with their efforts.

'It's coming along,' Mr Hope said cheerfully.

'We've brought you a drink,' said Ben, brandishing a big plastic bottle.

'I could do with a break,' Mr Hope admitted.

'Me too,' Mandy agreed. She scrambled up the bank. 'James, will you give me a hand with the picnic?'

James finished kicking the log he was holding into place, then joined Mandy as she bent down to open the hamper. They began spreading out the sandwiches and fruit. Just then, Mandy noticed that the sky had darkened. A bank of cloud had moved in from the west. It covered the morning sun and the sudden cool was welcome.

Sue sat down on the grass and crossed her legs.

There was a distant rumble of thunder and she looked up at the sky. 'Typical,' she commented, rolling her eyes. 'It's going to rain, just in time for our picnic.' Daisy sat beside her. She stretched forward her back paw to scratch the knot of string that tied the lampshade to her collar.

'We should remove that lampshade in the next day or so,' said Adam Hope, watching Daisy.

'She's had enough of it,' Ben agreed. 'Her wound looks pretty much healed now.'

Blackie came up from the river to join Daisy. He shook the water from his coat, showering Daisy with muddy droplets. She went over to say hello, trying to sniff at Blackie's damp coat, but the cone kept her from getting close enough.

Mandy passed James an apple. He was looking at all the goodies they'd unpacked from the hamper, then put out the palm of his hand as the first big drops of rain began to fall.

'Uh-oh...' Mandy said. She had taken a can of coke out of the basket, but thought better of it and put it back.

'Those clouds look fairly menacing,' said Emily Hope. She threw down her trowel and climbed up to the top of the bank. 'We'd better call it quits for now. I don't fancy getting any muddier.'

'I'll take the basket,' Mr Hope volunteered. 'Let's go.'

Everybody scrambled for cover as the rain came lashing down. The leafy branches of the trees were bowed with the weight of the downpour and Mandy shrieked as a cold shower of water slithered down the back of her neck.

'This is a shortcut,' shouted Sue, beckoning down a narrow path as she sprinted ahead. 'Follow me.'

Pounding along in her muddy trainers, Mandy noticed Otto and Splash in their pool. They were taking full advantage of the weather, rolling about in the water with evident glee. At least someone was enjoying the rain, she thought.

The enforced break from rebuilding the holt gave Mandy a chance to spend time with Belle. While the others shared the picnic in the kitchen, she took her apple and slipped away.

Belle was asleep but she woke up when Mandy peeled back the blanket that was draped over the crate to keep out the light. She knelt down, her chin on the table. It was thrilling to be so close to the little animal. Belle shrunk away to the far end of her crate, but kept her brown eyes trained on Mandy. Her nose twitched.

'Sweet girl,' Mandy murmured. 'How are you feeling?'

Belle blinked and made a small chattering sound. She looked round the room, but her eyes came back to rest on Mandy's face. Mandy spoke to her in a soft voice, keeping very still. The otter's eye seemed less swollen and, as Mandy sat there, Belle suddenly rolled over on to her back. Clasping her front paws over her pale furry chest, she looked at Mandy from upside down. Mandy was pleased. It seemed a very trusting thing for the otter to have done and Mandy was sure Belle was feeling more relaxed.

'Mandy?' The door to the utility room opened and Belle turned over and backed into a corner. Emily Hope looked in. 'We *did* pack the cheese sandwiches, didn't we?'

'Yep,' Mandy nodded. 'I put them in the basket after I'd wrapped them in foil.'

'Well, they're not there,' said Mrs Hope. 'Are you sure?'

'Absolutely certain!' Mandy thought for a moment, then she grinned. 'Blackie?'

Mrs Hope covered her face with her hands. 'Oh, no!'

Mandy drew her mother's attention to the otter. 'Mum, Belle seems much better. She seems a little playful, even. Do you think she's ready to go into an outside pen?'

'She does seem better,' said Emily Hope, taking a look. 'That's good news! I'll speak to Sue and Ben about the possibility of releasing her. Will you come and give us a hand with making a new round of sandwiches?'

'OK,' said Mandy, leaving Belle rather reluctantly.

In the kitchen, James was gazing sorrowfully at his dog.

'I know I packed the sandwiches, James, so Blackie must be the thief,' Mandy told him.

'Yep,' James agreed. 'Took them from right under our noses!' Blackie looked up at his owner with loving eyes. 'And I'm *starving*, too. What am I going to do with you!'

'It must have been Blackie,' added Adam Hope. 'Daisy couldn't have reached into the basket wearing her cone.'

'Bad dog!' James said sternly.

'Never mind.' Sue laughed, holding up one hand. 'Let's make more sandwiches and say no more about it. Poor Blackie always seems to be in trouble.'

The Labrador seemed hurt by James's tone. He slunk away and curled up very close to Daisy on the hearth rug. He put his nose on to his front paws, but kept his eyes on James. Mandy thought he looked very apologetic.

'Sue,' she said, turning to wash her hands at the sink, 'can we take Belle out of that cage? She really is better.'

'I thought so too,' Sue replied, as she sliced into a hunk of cheese. 'But we don't have a spare outdoor enclosure and she isn't well enough to go free just yet. She hasn't finished her course of medication.'

'Best to keep an eye on her for a while longer, even if she does have to stay in that cage,' Mr Hope advised.

'I've got an idea!' Ben's face lit up. 'It's a bit of an experiment though . . .' He trailed off.

'What?' Mandy was dying to know what Ben was thinking.

'Well . . . how about . . . no, maybe it's too soon.' He rubbed his chin, looking thoughtful.

'Tell us,' urged Sue, looking puzzled. 'What's your idea, Ben?'

'I don't know if it'd work . . .' mused Ben. 'But what about putting her in with Sprite?'

'Yes!' Mandy burst out. 'It's a *wonderful* idea. Belle could be just what he needs!'

Ben grinned at Mandy. 'That's exactly what I was thinking!' he said.

'Belle and Sprite?' Sue sounded hesitant. 'Together . . . as mates?'

'He's so lonely,' Mandy pointed out. 'And she's alone, too. If they get along well, they might team up together and have a family.'

'More otters for the river,' said James. 'That would be terrific.'

Sue and Ben exchanged glances, then they smiled. 'A mate for Sprite!' Sue said. 'It's a long shot, but it's worth a try!'

Eight

Mandy was so excited about the possibility of the two sad otters making friends, she could barely sit still long enough to finish what was left of the picnic. She excused herself from the table and went to see Belle.

James followed. 'You're right. She's looking much happier,' he announced.

Instead of trying to hide, the otter waddled up to the wire, her broad black nose nuzzling it curiously. Mandy was tempted to try and touch her, but she knew that getting the little animal used to humans would not be helpful. Belle stood on her hind legs and put her furry paws up on the bars. She gave a small cry and braced her sturdy little arms against the barrier.

Mandy's heart melted. Poor little creature. One moment she was running free, her knowledge of humans non-existent, now here she was cooped up in a small wire pen.

'It won't be long,' Mandy told her. 'You're going to be out of here soon and swimming along in the river.'

'Not quite yet.' Sue and Ben, with Mandy's parents, had come into the room to examine Belle. Mandy and James moved out of the way to let them get closer to the cage.

'The swelling has gone down,' said Mrs Hope. 'She seems more active, too.'

'Can we put her in with Sprite, do you think? Today, I mean?' asked James.

'I think we should try and introduce them to each other gradually,' Sue replied.

'Let's roll a stretch of chicken wire across the middle of Sprite's enclosure,' Ben suggested. 'That way, Belle and Sprite can introduce themselves but still be separate.'

'That's a good idea,' agreed Adam Hope. 'We don't want to rush them.'

Ben looked out of the window. The rain had

slowed to a fine drizzle and the clouds were clearing. 'I'll need a hand, if you don't mind, Adam?'

Mr Hope pulled on his jacket. 'Sure. Emily, will you and Sue bring Belle down to the holt in a while?'

'Oh, great!' Mandy's eyes were shining. 'You mean now? Good! James and I will help.'

'Put your boots on again,' Sue advised. 'When we've settled Belle, we must get on with rebuilding the river holt, if we can. There won't be a chance to do much around here tomorrow.'

'Oh? Why not?' asked Mrs Hope, as she gathered Belle's medication.

'Ben's going sailing!' Sue grinned. 'He's taking part in a regatta on the lake.'

'Wow!' said James. 'That'll be fun.'

Sue smiled. 'You're welcome to join us, if you like. I think it *will* be fun – if the weather is OK.'

'Adam has always wanted to take part in a boat race,' Mrs Hope chuckled. 'He'll be thrilled to come along and lend a hand.'

'We'd love to have you!' said Sue. As she lifted the holding cage, Mandy's mum had a good look at Belle's eye.

'It's looking fine,' Emily Hope said.

'Great.' Sue smiled. 'Now, let's get this young lady down to meet her prospective partner!'

'Can we carry her?' asked Mandy.

'Sure,' Sue replied.

Belle in her wire cage was heavier than Mandy expected. Her heart went out to the little animal as she heard her whimper and mewl nervously.

When they arrived, Adam Hope and Ben had just finished securing the mesh wiring across Sprite's holt. The enclosure was now neatly divided in half. Sprite had retreated into the farthest corner of the pen. He backed in among a tangle of twigs and logs at the edge of the river, looking glumly at the crowd gathering around the perimeter of his pen.

Mr Hope opened the gate and Mandy and James inched inside. They lowered the cage gently to the ground and went out of the pen. For a moment, Belle panicked and scooted from corner to corner of the crate, trying to find a way to escape. Then Sue leaned over the fence to undo the clip and the door swung open.

Belle lifted her head. Sprite's scent made her nose quiver with interest. She waddled out on to the earth floor of the riverbank and looked around her slowly. Then, spotting the hollow log, she hurried for cover.

'Let's leave them alone together,' said Ben. 'They'll need time to adjust.'

'Right,' Mr Hope nodded. He flexed his arm muscle playfully. 'Who's for a spot of holt building?'

'Me,' said Mandy, a little disappointed that Belle had bolted into the log. She would have liked to stay and watch the otters, but she knew they'd be more relaxed alone.

'Me too,' James nodded.

'We'll need to finish the holt today if we want to go in for that race tomorrow,' Mandy added.

'Race?' echoed Adam Hope, his eyebrows raised. 'What race?'

'It's a regatta,' Mandy's mum explained. 'On Windermere. The Sullivans are taking part and have asked us to join them.'

'That's *fantastic*.' Adam Hope smiled broadly. He looked at Ben and Sue. 'It's something I've always wanted to do!'

'Good,' said Ben. 'It's the least we can do to thank you for all the help you've given us. Are you an experienced sailor?'

'Um . . . no,' Adam Hope confessed. 'But I'd like to give it a try anyway.'

'Done!' Ben laughed and slapped Mr Hope on the back.

'Let's finish repairing the river holt before we even *think* about sailing a boat,' Emily Hope cautioned. 'We need to be ready for the council's inspection.'

Mandy stood up and brushed down her jeans, knowing just how important it was to get to work on the holt right away. Perhaps Sprite and Belle would be the first occupants, as the first safe step on their way to freedom. It was a lovely thought and Mandy had a spring in her step as she followed the others to the river.

By late afternoon, the river holt had its split pole roof in place, and the network of pipes was laid in the ground below. Adam Hope and James had reinforced the mud walls with stones and sticks, to guard against another collapse. Once again, it looked like a perfect little haven for Lakeside's otters.

'This could even be a hotel for otters passing by,' James remarked, dabbing at perspiration on his forehead with the sleeve of his T-shirt.

'As good as new,' Mandy said with satisfaction.

'I can't thank you enough,' grinned Sue. 'Really, you've done wonders.'

'Sue and I would have had to work around the clock to complete this in time,' agreed Ben. 'You've been absolutely wonderful – all of you.'

Blackie wagged his tail as though he understood and Sue laughed. 'Well, I'm not so sure about *you* being a great help!' She ruffled his head.

'Now, go home, all of you!' Ben pleaded, grinning. 'You deserve a long rest. You'll need all your strength if we're going to win that race tomorrow.'

Mr Hope's face lit up. 'I'm looking forward to that,' he said.

'We'll walk with you back to your car,' Sue suggested. 'Ben can give you directions to our mooring before you leave.'

'Can I check on Belle before we go?' asked Mandy.

'Go ahead,' nodded Ben, as he gathered the muddy tools together.

Mandy and James dashed along to take a peep into Sprite's pen. There was no sign of Belle and Sprite hadn't moved since they had last seen him. He was in exactly the same position, in among the branches, with only his sad little face visible.

'Oh dear,' muttered James. 'It doesn't look so good, does it?'

'She'll come out of that log when she's ready,' Mandy said encouragingly. She wondered about lingering a while to watch the otters, but the thought of a hot shower and something to eat made her suddenly eager to get home. 'I'm sure they're going to be great friends. We'll find how they're doing from Ben and Sue tomorrow.'

Emily Hope groaned as she got out of the car at the river the following morning. 'Every bit of me hurts after all that earth-moving,' she said.

'Me too,' James nodded sympathetically and rubbed his upper part of his right arm. 'Especially this muscle here.'

'And my back aches,' added Mr Hope, unloading their picnic from the back of the car. 'All that digging . . .'

Mandy chuckled. 'Listen to you lot!' she said. 'We're not going to be much use to Ben and Sue in this state!' Blackie had found a ball in the car and dropped it at Mandy's feet, looking up at her hopefully. She threw it for him and he bounded off happily to retrieve it.

A hundred metres downriver from where they were unloading the Land-rover, Mandy could see a small boathouse and a concrete launch strip sloping into the water.

'Maybe that's Ben and Sue's boat?' said Mandy, pointing.

'Why don't you go and see?' suggested Mrs Hope.

Blackie, still holding his ball, was hard on Mandy and James's heels as they ran along the bank and down the launchway to where a small yacht bobbed alongside the riverbank.

'*Tarka,*' Mandy read the name inscribed on her hull. 'That was the name of the otter in the book I read! This *must* be the Sullivans' boat.'

A dog barked and Mandy saw Blackie drop his ball and stare at the yacht. Then a golden nose shrouded in a lampshade appeared on deck.

'Daisy!' Mandy cried. The Labrador wagged her tail.

The boat was about five metres long and her sail was folded round a tall wooden mast. At the far end of the deck, Ben was busying himself with the mooring line, coiling a long length of thick rope round one arm.

'Ahoy there!' he shouted, and waved. Daisy jumped rather clumsily off the boat and scampered towards Blackie. Her lampshade rattled and shook as she ran and the two dogs greeted each other as though they hadn't seen each other in days.

Sue was sorting through some lifejackets tangled in a box in the boot of their car, which was parked beside the boathouse. She smiled at Mandy and James as they went over to greet her. 'Hi, you two. These ought to fit,' she said, passing them over.

'Thanks,' said James, taking one and passing the other to Mandy.

'Thank you,' Mandy said. It was a hot day, and she thought she would hold off putting her lifejacket on until the last moment.

'Is there one for me?' Adam Hope strode over, grinning. 'And Emily?'

'Absolutely,' smiled Sue.

Ben and Mr Hope were keen to be off, so Mrs Hope and Sue began to hand their combined supplies to James and Mandy to carry on board. Then, Mandy and James, the four adults and the two dogs gathered to hear Ben's plan.

'We'll use the outboard motor to travel upriver,'

he said, 'then stop and have a picnic lunch within easy distance of the regatta's starting point.'

The dogs swirled around excitedly, getting in everyone's way as they prepared for departure. The yacht was a bit crowded, so Emily Hope and Sue offered to walk along the bank with the dogs, giving Daisy and Blackie a good long run and leaving room for the crew. Daisy was hardly limping at all now, and she seemed filled with energy and excitement.

Tarka's outboard engine was fired up and they set off in the direction of the mouth of the river. With Ben at the helm, the boat puttered along under the trees and Mandy scanned the riverbank for any signs of otter holts. This was perfect otter territory, she was sure, and she hoped she might spot a furry head and beady eyes popping up from a hole in the bank.

Looking upriver to where it opened out into the lake, Mandy could see a billowing rainbow of brightly coloured sails, flapping in the breeze. Snowy-white hulls of boats of varying sizes were making for the starting line, marked by buoys.

James yelled to his dog as *Tarka* gathered speed towards the lake. Blackie pricked up his ears and ran to the water's edge. For a moment, Mandy

thought he was going to leap into the river and swim after James. Sensibly, the Labrador chose to race along the bank, barking loudly, and keeping one eye on James out on the water.

By the time Ben cut *Tarka*'s motor and allowed the boat to drift up close to the riverbank, James and Mandy were ready for lunch. The fresh air had made them ravenous.

James was first off the boat. He made straight for the spot under some trees where Sue and Emily

Hope were opening plastic boxes filled with home-cooked food. Mandy followed him, shrugging off her heavy lifejacket to cool her damp T-shirt.

'That was great!' James puffed as he joined Mandy's mum and Sue. His glasses were askew on his nose and his trainers sopping wet. Blackie put his front paws on James's chest, leaving two muddy splodges on his white T-shirt.

'Can we have our picnic now?' asked Mandy, flopping on to the grass.

Mrs Hope laughed. 'Hungry?' she teased. 'You'll be even hungrier after the regatta!'

'Emily, have you seen a packet of cinnamon buns?' Sue frowned as she rummaged through the cool box. 'I know I put them in. They were right on the top of the hamper, wrapped in a paper napkin.'

'Oh, not again!' James groaned.

'Blackie!' Mandy gasped. 'You didn't! *Did* you?'

All eyes turned to the Labrador, who cowered under the stern looks he was getting. His tail curled between his legs and he slunk away to find a shady spot under a bush.

'Well, they're not here,' Sue finished, having turned out the contents of the cool box. The rest of the food had been laid out on the rug by now and Daisy came over to examine it all, wagging her tail gently. Then she sat down, and looked out over the lake, presenting a perfect, ladylike contrast to the greedy and badly behaved Blackie.

James looked mortified. 'I'm really, really sorry,' he said to Sue. 'I don't know what's got into Blackie.'

'Never mind,' Emily Hope smiled. 'We've got plenty of food. Nobody is going to starve.'

'Perhaps Mr Hope should fit a plastic bucket over Blackie's head,' James said to Sue. 'That would stop him thieving!'

Sue just shook her head in mild exasperation and waved over at Ben and Adam Hope, who were discussing something on board *Tarka*. 'Lunch!' she shouted.

Mandy couldn't help feeling sorry for Blackie. He seemed a bit bewildered and peeped out at them from under a leafy branch with a sad look on his face. He stayed where he was throughout lunch, and never once even ventured close enough to inspect the contents of the delicious-smelling picnic.

'Right.' Ben stood up and dusted the breadcrumbs from his shirtfront. 'Ready, crew?'

Mandy and James jumped up. 'Ready!' they said together.

Ben spoke purposefully. 'We'll sail together across to the jetty where the race will start. Then, Sue and Emily and the dogs will have to disembark. OK?'

'Aye aye, Captain,' grinned Adam Hope. He pulled on a peaked cap, and Emily Hope smiled at him.

Daisy picked up the shared excitement. She shook her head hard in yet another attempt to rid herself of the cumbersome cone. Then she went over to *Tarka* and jumped on board.

'Come on, Blackie!' Mandy clapped her hands to try and encourage Blackie to board as well but the Labrador still seemed miserable. He took his time, walking slowly towards *Tarka*, his head hanging. Then, at last, he jumped up on the deck.

'Good boy,' Mandy told him, stroking his head. Blackie flopped down, resting his full weight against Mandy's leg as she comforted him.

'He is not,' mumbled James. 'A good boy, I mean.'

Mandy took her lifejacket from Sue as everyone scrambled to find a place to sit. Grey cotton wool clouds were scudding across the sky and a breeze whipped the surface of the lake into ripples. Tarka began to creak and groan as the water swelled beneath her.

'Put your lifejackets on again,' Ben advised James and Mandy. 'It's one of the rules of the regatta – no sailing without lifejackets. Plus, it makes good sense now that we'll be sailing on the open water.'

The straps of Mandy's jacket had become tangled. Behind her, Adam Hope hoisted the main sail and it began to fill with the steady breeze. Tarka tilted into the wind and glided out towards the wider part of the lake.

'Lifejacket!' James reminded Mandy as he pulled his own jacket on.

'Mine's all knotted up . . .' Mandy muttered. Her hair had come loose from the clasp of her ponytail and was blowing across her face, making it difficult to see.

'I'll help you, love.' Emily Hope held out a hand and Mandy stood up to pass the lifejacket to her.

Just then, Tarka pitched sharply to one side. Mandy staggered backwards. She flung out a hand to steady herself – and the yellow lifejacket sailed free of her grasp and hit the water with a smack.

'Oh no!' yelled James. 'Lifejacket overboard!'

Nine

Mandy's lifejacket bobbed away on the water, just out of reach. Everybody stared after it, even the dogs. Mandy was torn. The water looked grey and choppy and she didn't fancy diving in, but without her lifejacket, she wouldn't be able to take part in the race.

Adam Hope snatched off his cap and began to take off his shoes. 'Looks like I'll have to go in after it,' he said cheerfully.

Ben quickly lowered the sail to slow the boat.

'I'm really sorry,' Mandy said.

But before Mr Hope had untied his laces,

Blackie leaped off *Tarka*'s deck and landed in the lake with an enormous splash.

Sue, who was standing nearest the rail, was drenched. 'Oh!' she spluttered. 'What is that dog up to now?'

'Blackie!' James shouted. He looked worried as well as cross. The water was deep and cold. Daisy fired off a volley of shrill barking. Her tail wagged madly, and Sue put a hand on her collar in case she decided to jump in after her friend.

But Mandy suddenly realised what Blackie was doing. 'Don't yell at him, James,' she urged. 'I think he's about to save the day!'

Blackie's smooth, powerful paddling helped him gain on the yellow lifejacket as it drifted in the current. He seized one of the floating cords with his teeth, then turned. The water lapped over his muzzle and he coughed.

'Good boy!' Mandy yelled, waving her arms in encouragement. 'Good, good dog!'

'Oh, Blackie . . .' Emily Hope laughed. 'We never knew you had it in you!'

'Come on, boy,' called James. He was smiling proudly. 'Here we are . . . come on.'

Blackie was breathing hard through his nose, keeping the strap clamped tight in his mouth. He blinked away the water in his eyes as he paddled back towards *Tarka*. At each enthusiastic shout from up on the deck of the boat, his ears pricked up.

Dragging his prize, Blackie reached *Tarka*. The deck loomed above his head, too high for him to climb in. Ben Sullivan grabbed at the lifejacket and Adam and Emily Hope reached down to help Blackie aboard. Sue hung on to Daisy, who was quivering with the effort of trying to break free.

With a great thud, a very wet Blackie was hauled on deck. In spite of how wet and cold he was, Mandy hugged him and planted a kiss on his dripping nose. Everyone cheered loudly and reached out to stroke the black Labrador. Again and again he shook himself, sending droplets of water flying in every direction.

'What a hero!' James declared, wiping his face with the palm of his hand.

Sue accepted a long lick up her arm. 'You're a very clever boy,' she told him.

'You've saved the day, Blackie, but if we don't get a move on, we're going to miss the start of the race. We'd better get going!' Ben handed Mandy her soggy lifejacket and she put it on with a grimace. At least she'd be able to take part in the race now, thanks to James's talented dog!

By the time *Tarka* arrived at the small jetty sticking out into the lake, Mandy could tell that Blackie and Daisy were more than ready to go ashore. A game of tag on deck was out of the question, and both dogs seemed to be longing to play. They jumped ashore after Mrs Hope and Sue, and Daisy's bobbing lampshade soon drew lots of attention from the spectators gathered to watch the race.

'Wow!' breathed James, looking out at the boats spread across the water. Most were small yachts, like *Tarka*. Sails were hoisted as they jostled into position, ready to start. Mandy spotted a lovely little boat with the name *Belle* painted on her stern. Her thoughts flew to the otter, and she wondered how she and Sprite were getting on.

But there was no time to worry about the otters now. Ben was seated at *Tarka*'s stern. He had one hand on the tiller and the other holding a length of rope that controlled the angle of the main mast. A shot rang out from the starting pistol and Mandy jumped.

'Cast off!' cried Ben.

'Best of luck, *Tarka*!' Sue called, and Emily Hope blew Mandy a kiss.

A second later, *Tarka* was gliding forward. She reared up against the swell, pushed along by the wind, and then began tacking from side to side. The water made a creamy froth in the boat's wake and Mandy felt a thrill run up and down her spine. She waved to a girl on the deck of the dinghy closest to them. The girl waved back.

'This is great!' Mandy shouted to James, who nodded. His cheeks were pink with excitement and his hair was standing up in the wind.

The lake widened, then narrowed and Ben and Adam Hope sailed *Tarka* deftly towards the first of the buoys that marked the course of the race. Mandy loved the way the sail billowed and filled with the rush of air. The cream-coloured canvas was so taut she thought it might tear open at any second.

Tarka gathered speed and drew ahead of the dinghy called *Belle*. The first buoy was upwind of their starting point and they reached it easily.

Adam Hope gave a whoop of exhilaration. 'Watch out for the boom,' he shouted to Mandy and James. He pointed to the sturdy wooden beam holding the sail to the mast. 'When the boat changes direction, it will swing right over your heads.'

As he spoke, Ben Sullivan changed course, pulling hard on the tiller as he made for the second buoy. The boom swung round and Mandy only just managed to duck her head in time. James put his head on his knees and Mandy heard him chuckling.

Now *Tarka* was hard on the stern of the boat in front of her. But with the shift in the wind, Ben couldn't get past. *Tarka*'s speed began to drop.

'Oh, no!' cried Mr Hope. 'We're losing our place, Ben.'

'That dinghy is taking our wind,' Ben yelled back.

Then there was another change in the gusting wind, and *Tarka* began to overtake the boat ahead. Mandy's heart thumped as the yacht lurched from side to side. The water splashed up on deck, soaking Mandy's trainers and socks. They were going really fast now, zipping through the marked course and heading for the finish.

'Where does the race end?' asked James, leaning to shout into Mandy's ear.

She pointed. 'Over there – where you can see

that motor boat. Those are the judges in it.'

'Oh!' said James, and fixed his eyes on the motor launch up ahead. 'Come on, Mr Sullivan, Mr Hope,' he shouted. 'We can do it!'

The wind carried *Tarka* towards the finish, and for a moment, Mandy thought they were going to win.

'Nearly there!' she cried, and the wind whipped the words out of her mouth. Ben and her father were concentrating hard. There was just one boat left in front of them – a brightly coloured yacht that had rounded the sixth buoy and was steaming for the finish.

Mandy willed *Tarka* to go even faster. She could clearly see the two judges in the motor launch now. She ducked as the boom swiped cleanly across her head, then sat up, just as the brightly coloured yacht crossed the finish line ahead of *Tarka.*

'Second!' she shouted, tugging at James's sleeve. 'We came second!'

A cheer went up from the spectators on the shore. Adam Hope was grinning from ear to ear. He shook Ben's hand and laughed as the sail came down.

'What a crew!' panted Ben, patting James and

Mandy on the back in turn. 'Well done, team!'

Mandy was thrilled. She spotted her mum on the jetty, jumping up and down. She waved back and gave her a thumbs-up sign.

'That was fantastic,' said James.

'It was!' Mandy agreed. She turned to her father and gave him a hug. 'What a sailor! Well done, Dad.'

Tired as she was when they arrived back at Lakeside, Mandy was itching to see Sprite and Belle.

'I'll take that cone off Daisy now,' said Mr Hope, dumping the hamper on the kitchen counter.

'Oh, great,' said Mandy. She was longing to see Daisy's pretty face and bright eyes properly again.

Sue was making a pot of tea and Mrs Hope was unloading the remains of the picnic from the hamper. Daisy and Blackie were lying side by side under the kitchen table, dozing.

Suddenly, Daisy stood up and Mandy saw her black nose begin to twitch. She followed the scent she had picked up, right to the kitchen table. Before Mandy could think about what Daisy was doing, the golden Labrador was standing on her hind legs, her forepaws on a chair. In one swift, expert move, she raised her good paw to the table and dragged a leftover sandwich towards the lip of the upturned bucket. The sandwich dropped neatly into the cone. With a deft toss of her head, Daisy tipped it into her mouth and gulped it down, her tail wagging nineteen to the dozen.

'Daisy!' Mandy pointed an accusing finger at the Labrador, her mouth open. 'It was you all along!'

'What was?' Emily Hope turned.

Mandy, trying hard not to laugh, explained what she had just seen. It looked like Daisy had found a way to steal food in spite of her cone!

'Clever,' remarked James with a wry smile. 'So who's been a bad influence on whom, I wonder?'

'Poor Blackie has been wrongly accused,' said Sue, stooping to stroke Blackie's head.

Mrs Hope laughed. 'And you looking as though butter wouldn't melt in your mouth, Daisy!'

Blackie wagged his tail, delighted by all the friendly attention he was getting. When Mandy's father arrived to cut through the knots on Daisy's collar, Mandy told him about the nifty theft of the cheese sandwich and he roared with laughter.

'A very stealthy thief!' he remarked. 'Who would have thought that a lampshade would have come in so handy?'

The bright pink lampshade was eased off Daisy's head. Free of the clumsy cone, she went mad with joy. She shook her head for a minute to make sure it really had gone, and raced round the kitchen, knocking over a chair.

'Out!' pleaded Sue, flinging wide the back door. 'Out you go, the pair of you. What a circus!'

Daisy hurled herself on to the lawn and rolled over and over on her back, all four legs in the air. Mandy was so happy for her.

'I'm glad that's over,' said James, as though he had read Mandy's thoughts. 'Now she won't have to keep bumping into things.'

Mandy grinned. 'But I wonder if she'll miss it when it comes to stealing snacks? Now, come on, let's go and see Sprite and Belle!'

They approached Sprite's holt slowly and quietly. Mandy wanted to see the otters without being seen, so she and James crouched down and peered out from behind the camouflage of a handy bush. What she saw made Mandy's heart leap with joy.

Sprite and Belle were snuffling at each other through the wire mesh that separated them. Belle seemed to be making a careful examination of the male otter, starting with his face and working down the length of his body. Then she sat up, blinking curiously, and pushed at the partition with both paws. Sprite chattered back at her.

'She wants to get through to meet him,' whispered James.

'Oh, James, they've made friends!' Mandy breathed. 'Let's watch . . .'

With a jolt, Mandy realised it was the first time she had seen Sprite move about. The apathy and indifference were gone and Mandy was sure she could see a new brightness in the eyes that had seemed so dull before. He accepted the curious attentions of Belle, allowing himself to be thoroughly investigated by her nose and her paws. Then, in a gesture of submission, Belle rolled over on to her back. The top of her furry little head was pressed up close to the wire. Sprite put out a hesitant tongue and began to groom the bit of her he could reach.

'Oh!' Mandy was thrilled. 'Oh, how absolutely *fantastic!*'

The sound of approaching footsteps startled Belle. She shot away from Sprite and took cover behind a log. Sprite, who was used to the presence of Sue and Ben, stayed where he was.

'How're they getting on?' asked Sue in a low voice.

Mandy turned to her. 'We saw them snuggling up together at the wire—'

'And Sprite was grooming Belle,' James interrupted.

'They are friends already!' Mandy finished.

Sue nodded. A big smile spread over her face. 'That's very good news,' she said. 'Ben and I will keep an eye on them for a bit longer, then, tomorrow, we might put them into the river holt together.'

'Our last day,' Mandy said, feeling suddenly sad. Then she brightened. 'It will be a lovely last day and a really special end to our holiday if Belle and Sprite go back into the wild.'

'It will, Mandy,' agreed Sue. 'Now, your mum and dad are ready to go home. They're tired out. You'll have to say goodbye to the otters for now – until tomorrow.'

Ten

It rained all night, and Mandy woke up to the sound of gurgling water. She had been dreaming about the river carving its course through the Lakeside Otter Sanctuary and, for a moment, she couldn't think where she was. She went to the window and looked out. The sky was low and grey. Rain spattered against the glass.

Mandy remembered that today was their last in the Lake District. They were to spend it with Ben and Sue, and hopefully, would see Belle and Sprite make the river holt their new home. She pulled on a pair of mud-splattered jeans and took the stairs two at a time. She didn't want to miss a moment of being at the sanctuary.

James was tucking into an early breakfast while Adam Hope gave the little kitchen a final clean. Blackie sat beside the table, his gaze following the movement of James's spoon from cereal bowl to his mouth. He was drooling.

'Can you finish that cereal, James?' demanded Mr Hope. 'Blackie is dirtying the floor as fast as I wash it!'

'Sorry,' mumbled James. He took his breakfast out into the porch and Mandy grabbed an apple from the fruit bowl and followed.

'Remember,' she said, sitting beside him on the stone bench, 'the day we spotted Daisy lying right over there?'

James nodded. 'A lot has happened since then. It's been a busy week, hasn't it?' He made a face. 'Back to school, soon.'

Mandy nodded and took a big bite of her apple. 'It's been great, though.'

Blackie lay on the wet grass. He had a solemn expression on his face, as if he too knew that he would soon have to say goodbye to Daisy.

'It's been nice for Blackie to have a friend here,' said James.

'Maybe Daisy, with Ben and Sue, could come and visit us in Welford,' Mandy suggested.

James brightened. 'That would be excellent,' he said.

The kitchen door opened and Emily Hope looked out. 'Ready?' she called. 'We're going over to Lakeside now. We'll come back later to pack. Dad wants to get on the road by teatime.'

James and Mandy sprang up. Mandy gave Blackie her apple core and he crunched it happily. Then he followed them eagerly to the car, his tail waving in spite of the drizzle.

They found Sue and Ben down at Sprite's enclosure. The rain had stopped but Mandy could see that Ben had been working outside in spite of the wet weather, because his clothes were drenched. He was holding the wire cage that they'd used when Belle had been concussed. He and Sue were watching the pair so intently they didn't hear the Hopes and James approach.

'Hi,' Emily Hope said softly.

'Hello, all of you,' smiled Sue, turning. 'We've been watching these two all morning. They're great together!'

Mandy saw that the wire separating Belle and

Sprite had been taken down. The two otters were curled up, nose to tail. Belle's broad, silvery muzzle was buried contentedly in Sprite's thick fur. She raised her head and opened sleepy eyes at the sound of human voices. Mandy waited for her to lollop over to the hollow log for cover, but she didn't move. Instead, Belle blinked up at the crowd peering down at her, then idly began to groom Sprite's back leg.

'No sign of aggression?' asked Adam Hope.

Ben shook his head. 'Not for a second! It seems they've taken to each other in a big way,' he said. 'I'd like to think that, by next spring, they might have a family of their own.'

'How wonderful,' Mandy smiled.

'Sprite has eaten an enormous breakfast,' Sue reported. 'He scoffed up his fish and seems keen for more!'

'He'll find plenty of food in the river,' remarked Mrs Hope. 'And the challenge of finding it himself will do him good.'

'Right,' Ben agreed. 'Let's load them into the carrying cage and take them down to the holt, shall we?'

Mandy watched as Ben pulled on a pair of thickly padded gloves. He stepped into the holt, and Belle began to show signs of alarm. She waddled away from Sprite, making for the hollow log, but Ben caught up with her in a couple of long strides. He lifted her up, grasping the otter under her belly, and she let out a shriek of rage and fear. With one swift movement he had put the terrified otter into the cage. Belle thrashed about inside, calling to Sprite in a high-pitched squeal.

Mandy was sad to see Belle's alarm, but she knew that the treat that was in store for both otters would be worth the scary journey. Ben caught Sprite, who was more docile, with less trouble. His long, velvety tail hung down and swayed from side to side as he was lifted up and deposited in the cage beside Belle. They were a little crowded in there, but seemed to take comfort from being together again. Belle quietened down and stared round with huge dark eyes.

'Hurry, Ben,' Mandy begged.

Ben lifted the otters and walked quickly along the bank to the river holt. He strained at their combined weight, and Adam Hope hurried forward to take one side of the cage.

The river had swollen with the rain and it rushed and tumbled over the rocks, making noticeably more noise than it had before. The water level had risen and Mandy saw that it lapped much higher up the bank, half-filling the metal pipes laid inside.

Adam Hope and Ben slithered down the bank and landed with a dull splash in the muddy water. They pushed the cage deep inside the holt, so that the otters suddenly vanished from Mandy's view. She jumped down to the shore with James right behind her.

Ben reached inside and fumbled with the latch of the pen. The door swung open.

'Keep back,' Ben warned. 'Let's see what they do.'

Mandy crossed her fingers and wished hard. She didn't want Belle and Sprite to make straight for the river and quickly disappear. She hoped they would stay in their magnificent new home, and that she would be treated to the sight of them settling in. She waited and watched in silence, while the river water swirled around her boots, and the drizzly rain fell on her face.

Belle was first out of the cage. She stood aside politely to watch Sprite make his exit. Then, together they set about inspecting the excavation. Belle waddled about purposefully, peering into the pipes and turning over the stones Emily Hope and Mandy had laid there. Sprite stood up on his hind legs, reaching up to press at the log roof and chattering happily. Cautiously, he pushed his claws into the crevices between each carefully laid log, probing mysteriously for something only he understood.

'They're not going to swim away!' Mandy whispered to her mum.

'Not yet, anyway,' Emily Hope whispered back. 'They seem to like their new home.'

The otters explored the entire holt with great curiosity. They popped in and out of the pipes, and to Mandy it seemed as if, each time they emerged, they took comfort from the presence of each other.

Just when Mandy thought the pair might retire into one of the pipes for a nap, Sprite decided to lead Belle out to the river. Ben motioned to the others to climb back up on to the bank and, from there, Mandy had a great view of the otters' first taste of real freedom.

Belle made a soft chittering noise. She waddled into the swiftly flowing water and stood for a moment, looking up and down the stream. Sprite called softly to her in response, as though they were having a conversation about what to do next.

Then, together, they plunged into the water. Standing on the bank above, Mandy watched them glide like velvet brown arrows into the depths of the river. Sue and Ben hugged each other, and Adam and Emily Hope clapped their hands.

'They've gone!' said Sue.

Mandy saw that her eyes were bright with happy tears. 'Do you think they'll come back?' she asked.

'I'm sure they will,' Ben nodded. 'They've made their mark on this holt. They'll be back.'

Mandy looked down into the water, searching its depths for a final glimpse of Belle or Sprite. She felt sad and happy all at once. The otters had gone – and she didn't feel somehow as if she'd had enough time to say a proper goodbye. Her mother and father, with Ben and Sue, were walking away, chatting happily about the success of their first venture.

James stood silently beside her. 'They've gone,' he said, echoing her thoughts, and he too sounded sad.

'We should be happy,' Mandy told him. 'After

all, they're not pets. The whole point of rescuing them is to return them to the wild.'

'I know,' said James. 'But it seems as if they went too soon.'

Mandy knew exactly what he meant.

And then she saw them.

Sprite and Belle had hauled themselves out of the water a few metres downstream. The female otter shook her beautiful coat and scrambled up on to a rock sticking out of the water. Sprite joined her there.

Mandy gasped in excitement and clutched at James. Belle looked back at Mandy with a steady gaze, her warm brown eyes unblinking. Enchanted, Mandy held her gaze for several long seconds.

'Goodbye, lovely Belle,' she whispered. 'Bye, Sprite.'

The otters looked away, and dived gracefully into their watery world. And then they were gone.

Look out for more Animal Ark 2-books-in-1 Special editions . . .

PUPPIES IN PERIL

Animals aways come first for Mandy, and at Animal Ark – her parents' veterinary surgery – she is always making new friends.

PUP AT THE PALACE: On a visit to Buckingham Palace, Mandy spots a Labrador puppy, and then sees him again all over London. Who does the puppy belong to?

DOG AT THE DOOR: Mandy finds a pregnant Golden Retriever tied up outside Animal Ark, but no sign of her owner. Who could be responsible?